MURDER IN THE LAKES

AN ENGLISH MURDER MYSTERY

RACHEL AMPHLETT

Murder in the Lakes © 2025 by Rachel Amphlett

All rights reserved.

No part of this book may be reproduced in any form or by any electronic or mechanical means, including information storage and retrieval systems, without written permission from the author, except for the use of brief quotations in a book review.

This is a work of fiction. Names, characters, businesses, places, events, locales, and incidents are either the products of the author's imagination or used in a fictitious manner. Any resemblance to actual persons, living or dead, or actual events is purely coincidental.

CHAPTER ONE

It's never a good start to the day when the daughter of one of your clients leans across your desk and slaps you in the face.

She had a mean left hook on her too, helped somewhat by the platinum engagement ring that she'd only thought to remove after she'd hit me, before throwing it onto the carpet on her way out.

It helped – a little – that my client managed to hold back her smug look of satisfaction until after her daughter had stormed out of the office, slamming the door in her wake.

'I knew he was trouble, Melody,' she said. 'I told you.'

I stumbled around my desk, bent down to pick up the ring and handed it to Heather McAdams. 'Perhaps hang on to this,' I suggested. 'I'm presuming he'll want it back. Or you can sell it.'

I moved to the mini refrigerator under the window, cracked open the door and pulled out an ice pack.

I guess it shows how often this happens to me that I have one prepared.

I held the door to stop it swinging open. I didn't need my client to see the case of beer that Charlie had left in there on his last visit.

I held the ice pack to my cheek as I made my way back to my chair and somehow managed to sit down and look my client in the eye without losing my composure. My eyes stung, and I was going to have a bruise, that much was for sure.

Mrs McAdams only realised now how hard her daughter had slugged me, and that maybe I wasn't happy about it.

'Are you all right?' she said.

I glared at her. I had a sneaking suspicion her question was brought on by a sudden thought that her daughter might get sued for assault, rather than any concern for my welfare, and whether she should make a speedy phone call to the family solicitor.

'I'm fine,' I replied. 'I'll print out my invoice for you. I accept payment by card only.'

She looked taken aback for a moment, seemed to debate whether to ask if she could pay on account, and then thought better of it.

I ignored her and turned my attention to the computer screen instead. The system allowed me to automatically check off each service provided. I spitefully added an extra thirty pounds miscellaneous line item for the ice pack, hit the "print" button and then slid the still-warm invoice across the desk to Mrs McAdams.

'Oh, my,' she said, as she ran her manicured fingernail down the page. 'This is rather more than I expected.'

'A copy of my expenses is on the second page,' I said, jutting out my chin. 'I'm sure you'll find everything is in order. You'll appreciate that I do provide a rather exclusive service.'

She looked flustered. 'I wasn't implying—'

I raised an eyebrow.

She lowered her gaze in response and flicked over the page instead.

I drummed my fingers on the desk while she read through the numbers. Such a sign of impatience always annoyed the hell out of me when people did that anywhere within a mile radius of me, so I was banking on it getting on her nerves and that she'd hurry up and pay, then leave me in peace.

Sure enough, she flicked the page over with an exasperated sigh, then handed over her credit card.

It was from one of the larger banks, the word "platinum" embossed across the front of it with a sparkly finish that glinted in the sunlight streaming through the window.

A car horn honked somewhere beyond the double-glazed panes, followed in quick succession by a higher pitched *beep* and a stream of colourful swearing.

I swiped Heather McAdams's credit card across the handheld reader and handed it back to her, then used a large rubber stamp to punch the word "Paid" across the top of the invoice.

And yes, I pretended I was stamping her daughter's face with it before I released the spring mechanism.

'Thank you,' I said, and stood to show her the way out, dumping the ice pack on the desk. 'If you know of anyone else that would be in need of my services, please give them this.'

I handed over a business card.

Heather McAdams took it between her forefinger and thumb as if it was infected with weaponised smallpox and wrinkled her nose. 'I'd best go and find out where Charlotte is,' she sniffed.

I was careful not to slam the door behind her, such was my frustration. I put away the credit card machine, leaning against the cupboard door to lock it while last month's filing attempted to escape its clutches, and threw the remnants of the icepack in the waste bin in the small kitchenette off to one side of the open-plan office.

Then I wandered over to the window that overlooked the street below.

It was a fine day, a welcome change from the steady drizzle that had soaked the capital for the first two weeks of September. The puddles that had lined the pavements had evaporated, and one of the part-time employees from the café opposite my office window was wiping down the white plastic tables and chairs outside the doors in anticipation of a busy lunchtime.

Heather McAdams was hurrying across the road to an expensive-looking white cabriolet parked on the opposite side. Her daughter, Charlotte, was in the passenger seat, her arms crossed, fuming no doubt. An animated exchange began between the two of them as soon as Heather slid into the driver's seat, and they were still going at it as the car drove away.

I glanced at my watch.

It was only eleven-thirty, but I figured I'd earned an early lunch break, so I closed the office, flipped the cheery "Back Later!" sign over on the door, and walked down the internal stairs to the street towards the best sushi place in town, in my humble opinion. I grabbed a bento box, found a quiet corner of the restaurant to sit in, and picked up a fork.

I've never learned to use chopsticks. I've always been too hungry to bother.

As I tackled a particularly delicious piece of sashimi, I contemplated what I'd do for the rest of the day.

Contrary to what people might tell you, I am a private investigator. I've got the paperwork to prove it.

It was something I'd wanted to do since I was ten years old. My grandad used to lend me books about spies, detectives, and private eyes and I was enthralled by the stories of mysteries solved, righted wrongs and a pervading sense of justice. As a child, even playing hide and seek with my grandad – an ex-Royal Marines Commando – involved lessons in counter surveillance and being peppered with pinecones if he could spot my brother, cousin and me trying to hide from him in the woods.

I loved every moment of it.

That's why, when the world closed down a few years ago and I found myself abandoning a half-finished undergraduate degree like so many others, I decided to spend the time retraining. I found an online course, passed the exam a year later when the world reopened for business, and set out to follow my dream.

But when I first started out in my chosen role, actually *being* a PI was a career move quickly regretted when it became apparent that, at six foot tall, I stick out like a sore thumb, making covert work near impossible.

Not only that, but I also didn't have any police or military experience, so any would-be customers looked down their noses in disdain at my efforts to impress them with my qualification and karate black belt and then leave as soon as was deemed polite.

Sometimes they didn't even wait that long.

Distraught at my chosen career path disappearing down the nearest drain, I returned to my parents' house with the sole intention of moping around until I figured out what to do next.

That lasted precisely three weeks.

CHAPTER TWO

My grandad and I had always been close.

My earliest memories are of him pushing me in a wheelbarrow up the road towards the small allotment he tended to save him and my nan buying the weekly vegetables. While he ensured the tiny seedlings were watered, I was put in charge of pulling out any errant weeds that threatened his crop of carrots, potatoes, cabbages, and peas. We worked in silence, simply enjoying each other's company.

One day, a lady who rented a neighbouring patch of land came hurrying over to him, asking for his help.

Straightening, he'd rubbed his aching back, and then beckoned to me and we followed her over to where she'd erected a small shed.

'It's been eating all my bloody veg,' she'd said.

We looked to where she pointed, to see a baby rabbit cowering next to the shed, petrified by the sound of our voices.

The woman pointed at the shovel in my grandad's hands.

'Kill it.'

He baulked, and in that moment's pause, the rabbit took off, its white tail bobbing between the cabbages as it made a run for the boundary of the allotments.

'It got away!' The woman placed her hands on her hips and glared at Grandad.

'Sorry,' he said, and then jerked his head towards our patch. 'Come on. Back to work.'

As we wandered back towards our vegetables, I slipped my hand into his. 'I'm glad it ran away, Grandad.'

'Me too. I couldn't have killed it anyway.'

He looked down at me and winked, and in that moment I knew we'd become co-conspirators.

Even if he did pepper me with pinecones on a regular basis during our games of hide and seek.

Three weeks after I'd returned to my parents' house with no other accommodation options available, ruing the day I'd qualified as a private investigator, Grandad died peacefully in his sleep, leaving me wretched. I'd lost my best friend and confidant, and I didn't have a clue how I was going to cope.

Two weeks after that, and a week after his funeral, I was still struggling.

I dragged myself out of bed every morning, dressed, and thought I was doing okay – until I had to walk past his old armchair in the living room, the teak arms worn down by the palms of his hands over the years, and I'd fall apart again.

Mum suggested to me that I go for a walk every morning – more to get me out of the house I think, rather than any actual benefit. I'd return an hour or so later, completely unable to tell them where I'd been or what I'd seen.

I was numb.

It was a Friday morning when Dad found me in the dining room, absently scrolling through my social media news feed on my phone and wondering why the hell I was bothering.

'Thought I might find you here.'

I put down my phone and rubbed at stinging eyes.

He pulled out a chair at the end of the table

and lowered himself into it as if he was scared I'd bolt at the last minute. 'You've got to realise, Melody, your mum and I only want the best for you.'

I sniffed. 'I know, Dad. Really I do.'

'Well then, do something with your life. Stop moping around. I know you miss your grandad, but do you think he'd want to see you like this?'

'No.' Another loud sniff.

Dad shoved the box of tissues across the dining room table at me. It hit my elbow, and I tore two from the lid before blowing my nose loudly.

'You're not going to achieve anything sitting around here.' His tone softened, and I raised my eyes to meet his gaze.

'What do you mean?'

He reached into the pocket of his well-worn jeans and withdrew an envelope that had been folded in two. 'We had to wait until the solicitor had sorted out the will and everything before we could tell you. Before your grandad died, he made me promise that I'd pass this on to you, along with the message that came with it.'

I frowned, confused. 'What message?'

'Open the envelope first.'

I leaned over and took it from him, ran my thumb

under the seal and pulled out the thin slip of paper it held.

My eyes opened wide as I extracted a cheque. A very large cheque, with the solicitor's signature scrawled across the bottom right-hand corner. 'Dad?'

'Your grandad said, "Tell her to get out of here",' he said. His mouth twitched, and then he winked. 'I think he meant it in a nice way.'

'Oh, Dad.' I covered my mouth with my hand as tears rolled down my cheeks.

My grandad could still kick me up the backside, even from the grave, bless him.

It worked, though.

Four days later, I announced to my family and friends I was going to travel the world instead for a year while I sorted myself out and pondered what to do with my life.

However, after three months in Europe, I was running out of cash faster than my planned year break was passing by, and in an effort to make my money stretch a bit further, I booked a last-minute flight to Chennai, India.

I landed in monsoon season.

CHAPTER THREE

I loved India.

I loved the people, the food, the chaos – everything. And, while I was there, I found the inspiration for my new business.

Weddings are a big deal in the Indian community, no matter where in the world they live. I thought weddings in England were huge, but they were nowhere near as good as the ceremonies I saw in Chennai.

For a start, there's the explosion of colour – clothes swathed in reds, yellows, and bright oranges. Sometimes there are horse-drawn carriages sparkling with shiny tinsel and trinkets that jangle as the procession moves along the street accompanied by cheering from passers-by. Then there is the food, the customs, the way the whole community becomes involved and is consumed by the celebrations.

There's a lot of money involved in putting together a wedding, too. Families save for years leading up to the day their sons and daughters get around to tying the knot, and when you're spending that sort of money, you want to make sure you get what you're paying for.

That's where wedding detectives come into the picture.

A wedding detective will turn the prospective groom's life inside out, and all without him knowing.

Bank accounts, social media, career websites – nothing was off-limits to these entrepreneurial women.

As the twentieth century turned to the twenty-first, the old ways of arranged marriages were becoming shunned by a new generation of twenty-somethings who preferred informal matches to their parents' way of forging life partnerships.

With that came the inevitable suspicion and paranoia.

Who exactly *was* their daughter's groom?

How much money did he have? Where did he work? What was his lifestyle like? Did he have any unfavourable habits?

And, most importantly, would he be a good husband?

Pre-matrimony investigations uncover all of this and more, before being presented clandestinely to the future bride's parents for consideration.

Often, the private detective's work revealed nothing more than a late payment of a bill, perhaps an anomaly in an otherwise perfect credit history, or maybe a tendency to drink a little too much at work functions.

Sometimes, though, a scandalous indiscretion or a violent past was uncovered, and the wedding would be called off, saving the beloved daughter a lifetime of embarrassment – or worse.

Inspired, I spent the rest of my trip talking to the women that ran these businesses, learning from them, making pages and pages of notes, until one day I returned to Chennai airport and caught the next flight back to England to begin my new career.

If I couldn't be a private investigator, I'd be a wedding detective instead.

CHAPTER FOUR

When I returned from India, I discovered that Grandad had been even more generous than he and Dad had ever let on, which is how I found myself leasing a small office above a fish and chip shop in Bermondsey the second day after my flight landed back in the UK.

No, I have no idea why I picked Bermondsey either, and my only excuse for agreeing to be shown the office by the agent was that I was suffering from a crippling bout of jet lag.

As I traipsed up a narrow staircase and tried not to stare at his bum as I followed, I mentioned the smell of chip fat and fish that seemed to cling to everything.

'It's only the bins next to the window here.' He

waved his hand over his shoulder, as if to waft the thick aroma away. 'You won't notice it upstairs.'

I ran my hand over the stair bannister and immediately regretted my decision as it became covered in dust. I sneezed, wiped my hand on the back of my jeans, and tried not to panic.

What the hell was I letting myself in for?

The opportunity to bolt back downstairs and launch myself out through the door and into the street below was thwarted by the agent reaching the top of the stairs and turning to me with a key held aloft, a toothy smile creasing his features.

'The moment of truth,' he said, and swung open the door.

I managed to stop myself from gasping out loud.

Instead of the damp-ridden rat-infested garret I'd imagined, I stepped into an airy bright space that had been recently painted in modern neutral tones with white skirting boards, architraves and ceiling.

The floor had been stripped back to the original dark wooden boards and was polished to a high sheen, and as I walked over to the three large windows on the far side, I knew I was going to stay.

'What do you think?'

The agent's voice broke into my thoughts, and I

remembered my mum's advice about not appearing too keen.

I sniffed. 'I can still smell fish and chips.'

His nose puckered. 'Really? Oh, no. They assured me the new ventilation fans installed last week would sort that out.'

I felt bad, honestly I did, but Grandad's money wasn't going to last for long if I didn't haggle on the rent – and find some paying clients pretty quick.

I tilted up my head and sniffed again. 'The shop's open during the day too, aren't they?'

'From noon, yes.'

'Hmmm.'

I avoided his gaze and instead continued over to the window and rested my palms on the sill.

The view took my breath away.

Somehow, the building's original architect had ensured that its footprint managed to squeeze in between the jumble of shops and office blocks in such a way that the windows on the top floor offered an unobstructed view of Tower Bridge and the river, while at the same time providing a glimpse in between the green spaces that dotted the sprawling borough.

I don't know how I managed to stop my jaw from

hitting the floor, but I did manage to stop the squeak of surprise from escaping – just.

'Are you all right?'

The agent hurried over.

'Dust mites, I think. I'll be okay in a minute.' I gave a theatrical cough, patting my chest, and then jerked my thumb over my shoulder. 'The view's not bad.'

'I know,' he sighed, and joined me to stare at the vista. 'I'm told on a good day, you can see for miles.'

'A shame I won't have time to appreciate it,' I said, and began to pace the room. 'I expect I'll be too busy.'

I withdrew a tape measure from my bag and proceeded to work out where I would put a desk, chairs, visitor's sofa and rugs. To the side of the room, a small well-appointed kitchenette had been installed, and as I snapped the tape measure closed and ran my hand over the worktop that had been fixed in place, the agent cleared his throat.

'So, what do you think?'

I made sure I had a smile in place before I turned to face him.

'I'm sure if I were a software developer or something, it'd be perfect,' I said. 'Unfortunately, the sort of clientele I have demand confidentiality, and they're often from privileged backgrounds. They won't take kindly to having to approach the building from the street and then navigating such a narrow flight of stairs to reach me. And as for the smell—'

He automatically sniffed the air, and I bit back a laugh.

He held up a finger. 'Follow me.'

I did, and he led the way back to the small landing but instead of turning right to go downstairs, he turned left and opened a second door.

Bright sunlight poured in, and he stepped to one side to let me pass.

'It's only been used as a fire escape before,' he said. 'But perhaps if I persuaded the owner to have the ironwork repainted, and an alternative exit route established, you and your clients could use this instead?'

I moved past him and found myself standing on an ornate cast iron staircase that wound its way gently down the side of the building on the opposite side from the alley and into a narrow lane that thronged with life. A café bustled with energy nearer the entrance to the main street, while next door a new age shop displayed books and charms on white metal stands on either side of its front door. Beyond that, a little sushi bar looked like it was doing a busy late morning trade before the lane curved round and the next shop was out of sight.

Why the hell hadn't I noticed this on my way in?

What sort of detective was I?

'What do you think? Could this alternative entranceway work for your clients, do you think?'

I stepped back inside and waited while the agent shut the door.

Eventually I got my thoughts back in order.

Haggle.

'I suppose it'll have to do, yes.'

'Excellent.' He smiled. 'Now, in respect of the rent.'

'Yes, that. Well, I—'

He interrupted me again by holding up a finger. 'I realise the cooking aromas may be a little off-putting to your clients, and there's the hassle of having to use this alternative entrance,' he said. He lowered his voice. 'But, between you and me, the owner has been a right pain in the arse to deal with.'

My eyebrows must've shot upwards, because he smiled.

'How about we say an initial weekly rent for the first three months, then increase to a moderately higher monthly rent for the rest of the calendar year? After that, well, we'll see how we're doing, shall we?'

Meaning, he didn't want the client placing the lease back on the books any time soon.

Meaning, if I was a good tenant, the place was mine for as long as I needed it.

Meaning, I had just scored office space for a fraction of the price I thought I was going to have to pay in this neighbourhood.

I thrust out my hand. 'I think we have a deal.'

CHAPTER FIVE

Having an office above a fish and chip shop wasn't all that bad, despite what I said to the agent.

The owners, Michael and Louise Zervas, comprised a second-generation Greek, married to a third-generation Irish Catholic. This had the effect that their two sons were mysterious as all hell but would then go and confess to their mother. Added to the intrigue was the fact that both were in their late twenties and, yes, I'll be honest – they weren't bad looking either, especially Charlie who was older than his brother by four minutes.

We soon formed a strong bond. The landlord was non-existent, the agent was happy so long as the rent got paid, and we were left alone.

Exactly what we all wanted.

The first two weeks of my tenancy were taken up with placing orders for furniture, ensuring the furniture turned up, and then rearranging it several times before I was happy with the overall result.

During this time, Charlie and Dan, his younger brother, proved to be invaluable.

It was like having two annoying older siblings around all the time. They offered to help lift heavy boxes up the stairs, put together furniture for me when I turned the air blue while stomping around with a screwdriver, and would have moved in if I hadn't said quite firmly at the end of the two weeks that I was doing okay.

When Charlie found out what my new business was, he became incredibly concerned, exactly as I expected an older brother would.

'Have you any idea the sort of people that you're going to come into contact with?' he said.

'Of course. You're forgetting, I shadowed women doing this job in India. If they can do it there, I'm more than capable of looking after myself here in London.'

Charlie didn't look convinced. 'I really think you ought to think about getting some security cameras on the stairs and on your front door. One in your office as well.'

'I can't. There's no point having a business that guarantees client privacy if there are CCTV cameras all around the place, is there?'

'Okay, then I'll have to keep an eye on you,' he said, and began air boxing and kicking at an invisible opponent. 'I can protect you. Black belt Shotokan. Blue belt hanbō.' He stopped and grinned.

'You're not a ninja, Charlie. You help run a fish and chip shop. Besides, last time we sparred, I kicked your arse.'

I smiled at the memory and then stabbed my fork into the last piece of sashimi in the bento box as my thoughts turned to what on earth I was going to do now that the work for Heather McAdams was over.

It's hard to get recommendations in a business where your job is to expose the sordid backgrounds of your clients' future in-laws. They're either pleased that you've uncovered nothing but won't tell their nearest and dearest what you've done to ensure that, or they're dealing with the fallout from my investigations and trying to patch up their relationship with their broken-hearted offspring.

Such as this morning's client.

When I started out, I found my first clients with a bit of savvy, paid social media advertising, and my friends spreading the word. Whether my friends were simply foisting people onto me in sympathy, I don't expect I'll ever know, but it was appreciated. I proved I could be discreet, confidential, and – when the worst happened, and I did find out something unsavoury about someone's potential husband or wife – benevolent.

The first part of my role as a wedding detective was to conduct a search on social media. You'd be amazed at how many people do some really dodgy stuff, post it online for a drunken laugh, and then forget about it.

You'd also be surprised how many people don't set their privacy settings so only their friends can see what they post. You only need another friend or acquaintance to tag you, and everybody else can see it. And see your indiscretions.

Next, comes the financial searches. A lot of my clients want to make sure that their daughters or sons aren't being snatched up by a money-grabbing predator. Prenuptial agreements will only protect them so far.

Finally, if I *am* suspicious about anything, I'll carry out some covert surveillance. Usually that's done from a distance, nothing like what you see in spy movies, and very rarely do I need to use the GPS tracking devices I keep under lock and key in the office.

Much to Charlie's disappointment.

Of course, often I don't find anything, and the wedding goes ahead – it's only in extreme cases that I find something, and the wedding is called off – like the one I just gained a black eye for.

I hoped Charlotte McAdams recovered from the shock of finding out her fiancé of eight months hadn't yet divorced his second wife – the one he hadn't told her about – but my cheekbone still smarted, and I had no new bookings in the diary to make a start on back at the office.

I sighed and closed the empty bento box, then pushed back my chair and squared my shoulders as I left the sushi bar.

The day could only get better, right?

CHAPTER SIX

The afternoon passed by without so much as a murmur from the phone, and after checking my emails for the nth time, I was beginning to wonder whether I should've added another miscellaneous item to Heather McAdams's invoice.

I glared at the pile of receipts next to the laptop, remembering that my accountant was likely to fire me as a client if I didn't respond to his requests for more information so he could complete my tax return, and then heard footsteps on the metal staircase outside.

Shoving the receipts across the desk and into the top drawer, I slammed it shut at a tentative knock on the door before it opened, and a middle-aged woman peered in.

'Are you the private detective?'

'Like the sign says on the door, yes.' I rose to my feet as she walked in, pulling down my blouse and hoping she didn't notice the crumbs from the blueberry muffin I'd despatched fifteen minutes before tumble to the floor. 'I'm Mel – Melody – Harper.'

Her hand when she shook mine was bitterly cold, and limp. 'When it said Mel, I thought...'

I forced a smile as I led her to one of the armchairs beside my desk. 'The engraver got it wrong, and I keep meaning to change it, but—'

'I can imagine you're so busy, you haven't had a chance.' She took a seat and lowered her handbag to the floor beside her feet. She blinked. 'What happened to your face?'

'I, er, walked into one of the cupboard doors.' I flapped my hand towards the kitchenette as if I were swatting a fly. 'I told the builders they'd installed them at the wrong height.'

She didn't look convinced, but at least she had the decency to stop staring. Instead, she shifted in her seat, rummaged in her handbag, pulled out a mobile phone, and then replaced it before tugging a fresh paper tissue from a well-used packet and dabbing at her nose.

She sniffed.

I'd seen all the motions before from embarrassed or worried potential clients, and leaned forward, keeping my expression neutral.

'Ms—?'

'Patricia Berriminster. Mrs.'

'Mrs Berriminster, I can assure you that anything you say to me is held in the strictest confidence, even before we agree to terms and sign a contract. Tell me, what's troubling you?'

Her shoulders relaxed then, and it seemed like the stress left her features as she slumped in her seat.

Half my time as a private investigator is spent acting as an unqualified counsellor, but it helps – and it works. People open up to me, telling me their worst fears and suspicions, the secrets they can't discuss with their family for fear of ridicule or shame.

'Thank you,' she said. 'I feel so awful about doing this.'

'Most people do. I don't take it personally.'

She managed a small smile. 'If my husband found out, I don't know what he'd do.'

My senses were instantly alert at that point. I'd dealt with a few domestic violence cases before, and they never turned out well. I raised my fingers to my black eye, then thought better of it and leaned back, attempting a nonchalant posture. 'Well, he's not here and as a professional, I have my reputation to consider, so as I said, anything you say here is treated in confidence.'

'All right.' She took a deep breath. 'My daughter is getting married in ten days' time, and I'd like to find out more about my future son-in-law.'

I frowned. 'How long have they—'

'They got engaged four months ago. She's only known him for a year.'

'Where did they meet?'

'At an orienteering event.'

'Orienteering?' I wracked my memory. Didn't that involve maps and stuff?

'Oh, she really enjoys her hiking, and so about two years ago she joined a local group.'

'They do orienteering in London?' I couldn't help myself. I glanced out the window past the Bermondsey skyline.

'No, no,' Mrs Berriminster said, and wrinkled her nose. 'We're from Wiltshire. Marlborough, to be precise. Lots of good walking and fresh air there.'

I took the hint. Marlborough was evidently greener than Bermondsey.

'What's your daughter's name?'

'Natasha. Her fiancé is Ethan Kingsley. You might have heard of him?'

I shook my head in response.

Mrs Berriminster raised an eyebrow. 'His father is Seamus Kingsley, the online retailer. He made the *Times* top entrepreneurs list four years ago, you know. He's very connected.'

I flipped open my notebook and wrote down the details. 'And the orienteering event in Marlborough…?'

'It was a few miles away, near Fyfield Down country park.'

'Has Ethan done anything to give you cause for concern, or said anything that brings you here today?' I looked up from my scrawled handwriting to see Mrs Berriminster twisting her wedding band, her knuckles white. 'Is something the matter?'

'I really don't know if I should be talking about him like this,' she said. 'To you, I mean. Like I said, his father is Very Connected.'

I narrowed my eyes. 'In what way?'

'Politicians, chiefs of police, that sort of thing.'

'But you suspect something?'

Her shoulders slumped. 'Ethan was engaged before, and then suddenly he wasn't, and no one knows where his ex-fiancée is. She hasn't bothered posting to her social media profile or anything like that. It's like she's a ghost.'

'She may have simply created a different social media profile to create some distance between her and the Kingsleys. A lot of people do,' I said, before I looked down at my notebook once more. 'When is the wedding?'

'I told you. In ten days' time.' Mrs Berriminster picked at the tissue between her fingers, sending tiny fragments of two-ply confetti tumbling to the rug. 'Natasha is having her hen do this weekend, while Ethan is off to his stag weekend in Reykjavík.'

I saw a shiver clutch at her slim frame and leaned forward. 'It's certainly something I can help you with, Mrs Berriminster. I have access to a number of databases I can check over and above the usual search engines, and I can make some phone calls in the morning to some contacts of mine.'

'That's not good enough.'

'Pardon?'

She sighed. 'I'm sorry, but I need you to make sure nothing happens to Natasha between now and the wedding.'

'What do you mean?'

'I need you to go to the hen weekend.'

My jaw dropped. 'Go where exactly, Mrs Berriminster?'

'The Lake District, of course. She and her friends are doing a forty-eight-hour activities course. Archery, hiking, clay pigeon shooting, things like that.'

'But I don't know your daughter. I'm not going to be able to wrangle an invite at this late stage.'

'Oh, we don't expect you to go as a guest. That would be preposterous.' She managed a watery smile. 'I meant that you could pose as a staff member at the activities centre. I've already spoken with the owners. One of them owes me a favour after I sponsored a charity event there last year. They've said you can arrive at the centre before Natasha and her friends get there. That way, you can keep an eye on her while looking into Ethan's background at the same time, can't you?'

'Mrs Berriminster… Patricia. I'm a private investigator, like the sign says on the door. I'm not a bodyguard.'

Her bottom lip quivered. 'Please. I don't know who else to ask, and I'm worried. I'm scared my daughter is making an enormous mistake.'

I bit back a sigh.

It was only for a few days, I reminded myself. It

would pay the bills for this month, and I'd even have some money left over. Besides, it was an established activities centre with qualified instructors, and I'd only be expected to do what the more experienced guides there told me to do.

What could possibly go wrong?

CHAPTER SEVEN

The next morning found me in the Islington branch of a national camping equipment chain, my forehead creased while I stared at row upon row of sleeping bags, tents, backpacks and more.

There was a distinct aroma to the place, with fresh dyes and waterproof coatings from the various fleeces and base layers and jackets lining the rails mixing with the new leather walking boots displayed in racks over to the left of the store. More racks lined the aisle where I was standing, all of them laden with carabiners, ropes, water bottles, and more.

Uneven oak laminate flooring provided an appropriate rustic feel to the place, and there were posters lining the walls between the racks displaying men and women rock climbing, rafting and mountain biking. They were all wearing determined expressions, the latest in bright clothing, and were evidently fitter than me.

My heart sank as I stared at the notes app on my phone.

After Patricia Berriminster left my office the previous afternoon, I had spent the next three hours down a search engine rabbit hole while I researched first the activities centre I was going to, and then the sort of equipment a myriad of online experts recommended for weekend-long outdoor pursuits.

The subsequent list of purchases made my eyes water.

As far as preparedness went, I owned a pair of wellies with pink daisies that had last been worn at Glastonbury Festival three years ago, and a plastic waterproof poncho that had a London-based football team's logo splashed across the front of it. Neither would do for the sort of crowd that would be accompanying Natasha Berriminster to the Lake District.

I'd already been in the shop half an hour, doing my best to avoid the inquisitive glances the woman behind the counter was aiming my way, and side-stepping her older colleague while he unpacked a box of ski gloves and carefully labelled each pair before adding them to the rack halfway along the row.

It would have been easier to have visited one of the camping stores near my office, but people knew me there, and I didn't want anyone to latch on to the fact that I might be out of my depth.

My professional reputation depended upon it.

I lowered my phone with a sigh that must have been louder than I intended, because the man who had been unpacking the ski gloves straightened and turned to me with a concerned expression.

'Do you need some help?' he said.

My first instinct was to say no, but all I emitted was a frustrated squawk. I coughed, then managed a nervous laugh. 'I'm meant to be going on a wilderness retreat with some friends this weekend, but I've got no idea what to take and even though I've got a list of things I think I might need, I don't think I've got enough. Or maybe I've got too much. Or the wrong things, or…'

I clamped shut my mouth, feeling the heat rise to my cheeks.

He smiled, and the tanned skin at the corners of his eyes wrinkled. 'It can be a bit overwhelming when you first start out, can't it?'

MURDER IN THE LAKES

'Yes,' I said, relief sagging my shoulders. 'Can you help me?'

'Of course. Give me a minute to get rid of this.' He gestured to the empty box and brown paper packaging. 'I was about to make Lynn and myself a coffee. Want one?'

'Really? Um, milk and one sugar please.'

'Okay. Back soon.'

He gave me a wink before weaving his way between the racks towards the counter, murmured something to the woman – Lynn – who shot me a not unkindly smile – then disappeared through a door behind her.

I breathed out, feeling my heartbeat slow, and made my way over to the rails of walking trousers and fleeces, flicking through the hangers to find my sizes and wondering what the man... Flipping heck, I'd forgotten to ask his name.

'Here you go,' he said, appearing once more and brandishing two steaming mugs of coffee. He thrust one at me. 'I'm Will, by the way.'

'Thanks. I'm Melody.' I clinked my coffee mug against his and smiled. 'And thanks. You're right, I was getting overwhelmed. I've left it to the last minute as usual to get organised, and I have no idea where to start.'

'Okay, well – first things first. What activities are you planning to do this weekend?'

'According to the woman who's organised it for us, we're doing hiking, archery and clay pigeon shooting.' I shrugged. 'And I think we're camping overnight.'

'Do you know how much equipment is being provided?'

'All of the activities are catered for – we're staying at an adventure centre near Windermere. I've been told they're providing the tents and that sort of equipment. We just need to take sleeping bags, mats, that sort of thing.'

Will pointed at my phone. 'You were looking at that earlier. Has that got your shopping list on it?'

'Yes.' I sidled closer and held it up, angling the screen so he could see it before swiping open the notes app. 'I did some research online yesterday afternoon and came up with this.'

He reached out and steadied the phone, muttering under his breath as his gaze worked down the list, then grimaced. 'What's your budget?'

'Um…' I thought quickly. I couldn't tell him that Patricia Berriminster, my client, was going to be paying for my expenses, but nor did I want to appear ignorant. 'About three hundred pounds?'

Will dropped his hand and raised an eyebrow. 'You've got about twelve hundred pounds' worth of stuff on there.'

'Really?' I squeaked. 'Oh. But I've only got today to get all of this. I'm supposed to be leaving for the Lake District in the morning.'

He must have heard the desperation in my voice, because he used his coffee mug to gesture to the back of the shop. 'Follow me. We've been doing a stocktake ready for the winter collection to go out, and the sale items haven't been put on the racks yet. We might be able to help you out with some of this, at least.'

'Thank you.' I hurried after him and wondered if I would end up with clothes that left my wrists and ankles protruding by several inches.

Still, if they were cheap and kept me warm over the coming weekend, who was I to grumble?

Will led the way past colourful snowboarding jackets and eye-wateringly expensive goggles, then pointed to a jumble of clothing hanging from two portable stainless-steel racks. 'What size are you?'

'A ten, but I need—'

'Extra-long leg length. Yes, I can see that.' He said it without rancour, and after placing the two mugs on a nearby beech laminated counter, he stepped behind it for a moment and then bent down and dragged out a large box that had been stored there. 'These are men's sizes, but some of them didn't sell because they've got smaller waistlines. I reckon there'll be something in here to fit you. What do you need, a thirty-inch waist, give or take?'

'About that, yes.'

'Okay, I'll have a rummage. It'll be the same with the base layers over there on the rack – find something that's close to your chest size while I'm doing this, and you can try everything on in one of the changing rooms over there.'

'Brilliant, thanks.'

Almost an hour later, Will – and Lynn, who had found a pair of comfortable walking boots that cost a third of the original price in another box in a cupboard at the back of the store – were folding up my purchases and helping me check off the items from my list.

I was feeling a lot more confident than I had been when I first walked through the door, and somehow the sight of all that kit, including a head torch that Lynn assured me would be essential for nighttime toilet breaks, gave me a sense of quiet achievement. I hadn't been camping since an almost disastrous incident with the Girl Guide division I'd belonged to growing up, and despite my subsequent assurances to Patricia Berriminster when she had signed the contract between us, I had been approaching this assignment with trepidation.

Now though, I reckoned I was ready for anything.

Then my phone rang as Will was scanning the clothing tags into the till. I glanced at the screen, saw Patricia Berriminster's name on the display – well, the client code I'd assigned her for privacy, Mama Bear, which seemed fitting – and mumbled my apologies before moving over to the other side of the store to take the call.

'Hello, Miss Harper?' she chirped as soon as I answered. 'Are you in the Lake District yet?'

'Not yet,' I said. 'I'm leaving for Windermere in the morning. I emailed the manager of the activities centre, Chris, and he's going to pick me up from the train station. Why? Is there a problem?'

'Oh, nothing too serious.' She tittered. 'It's just that, well… I thought I'd better let you know. Ethan's mother is going to join the hen party.'

'Pardon?'

'Natasha's future mother-in-law. Isabella. She's decided she wants to join the girls this weekend, and Natasha thought it'd be a good idea to get to know her better, so of course she's agreed. I've only met

Isabella once or twice. She's very... rugged. Outdoors-y. Very good skier, apparently, and an excellent horsewoman. She's won a few competitions at a national level for eventing, that sort of thing.'

'Right, okay,' I said. 'Are you coming along as well?'

'Don't be ridiculous.' Her bark of laughter was so loud that I winced and held the phone away from my ear. 'I'm too refined for that sort of gallivanting around, Miss Harper. Besides, Peter and I are pruning the garden ready for winter this weekend.'

'Do you think Isabella's presence will cause a problem?'

'No... it's just that... well, I don't know how to say this, but Isabella will know straight away if you're not good enough. She must believe you're one of the activities centre employees. Do you see what I mean? You must ensure she doesn't find out what you're doing there.'

I did indeed, but I wasn't going to tell my client that.

'Not to worry,' I said breezily. 'I've got tomorrow afternoon and evening, and all day Friday to train with the centre's guides before Natasha's party gets there. I'm sure I'll pick up enough to get by.'

'Hmm.' Patricia didn't sound convinced. 'I

hope so.'

'Was there anything else, Mrs Berriminster?'

'No...'

'Then I'll be in touch as soon as I have anything to report.'

'Very well.'

She ended the call, and I took a deep breath before a polite cough from the direction of the counter caught my attention.

I turned to see Will and Lynn watching me expectantly.

'Everything okay?' said Will.

'Yes, sorry about that,' I replied, hurrying over and pasting a smile on my lips. 'What's the damage?'

'Only just over your budget,' said Lynn. 'Three hundred and fifteen pounds.'

I breathed a sigh of relief, despite seeing the four bulging bags I would now have to manoeuvre between the crowds on the Tube to get home, and swiped my bank card across the machine she held out. 'That's brilliant, thanks.'

'Good luck,' said Will, handing me the bags.

I thought of Ethan's mother, Isabella, and of the daunting task that Patricia Berriminster had set me. 'Thanks.'

I reckoned I was going to need it.

CHAPTER EIGHT

On Wednesday evenings, I had dinner with the Zervas family, no excuses.

Ever since my office had opened for business above their fish and chip shop, the Zervas family had insisted that I join them for dinner once a week, with Charlie the most vocal about the arrangement after he found out my own parents lived over eighty miles away in a sleepy Oxfordshire village.

Michael and Louise Zervas were full of energy for a pair of sixty-year-olds and worked all hours to make their fish and chip shop one of the most successful in the area.

Wednesday nights were for family though – including close friends.

They owned a terraced red-brick home that

offered a warm welcome, a friendly atmosphere, and great food. Apart from myself, they often invited friends to join them once a week to cook, eat, and share news. The open-plan living-dining room was always full of loud conversation, even louder laughter, and an eclectic selection of music thanks to Charlie and Dan arguing over their playlists like a pair of teenagers.

It was a twenty-minute journey from my tiny flat to the Zervases' house, but I'd invested in a 125cc moped on my arrival in London once I realised public transport had its limitations for a private investigator, and thankfully it wasn't raining.

I bumped my moped up the kerb and onto the concrete hardstanding in front of the front bay window and removed my helmet, ruffling my hair with my hand to get any wayward knots out of it. Popping open the top box behind the seat, I removed a hessian tote bag containing a bottle of red wine, my laptop and two travel memoirs I'd promised to give to Louise last time I was here and dropped the helmet into the space.

Locking it, I unzipped my protective jacket and crossed to the front door.

It opened before I'd had a chance to ring the bell.

'Have you lost your mind?' Louise demanded,

before dragging me over the threshold and shutting the door. She might have been a fraction over five feet tall, but she was strong from lifting all those bags of frozen chips and could bench-press more than me.

Ask Charlie.

'Hi, Louise,' I beamed, leaning down a little to kiss both of her cheeks. 'And no, no more than usual. I take it Charlie's told you about my trip up to the Lake District this weekend?'

'Just now, while he was helping me in the kitchen. Come on through. I want to hear all about it.'

I smiled and followed in her wake. I had lost count of how many times I'd said to Louise that I couldn't discuss my work due to confidentiality, but I had let Charlie know where I'd be – approximately – this weekend, so he wouldn't worry when I failed to appear at the office.

And Charlie had evidently told his mother.

He looked embarrassed when I walked into the kitchen, casting me a sideways glance from where he stood next to the hob stirring a delicious-smelling concoction in a large stainless-steel pan. He placed the wooden spoon to one side when he saw me and wiped his hands on a blue tea towel. 'Hi.'

'Hi.' I gave him a quick kiss on the cheek by way of greeting, then squealed as two enormous arms enveloped me from behind and lifted me off the ground. 'Dan, put me down. I haven't even taken my jacket off yet.'

Charlie's younger twin grinned when I turned to face him and held out his hand. 'Give it here, I'll go and hang it up. What's in the bag?'

I shrugged off my jacket and handed Louise the bottle of wine and the two books. 'Those are the ones I was telling you about. Feel free to pass them on – I'm running out of space in the flat and daren't keep them.'

'Thanks,' she beamed. Her brow puckered when she glanced down at the open bag. 'Is that your laptop?'

'It is. Please could I be cheeky and book my train tickets while we're talking before we have dinner? I ran out of time this afternoon, what with sorting everything else out, and I can't take my moped on the motorway. I'm hoping there are no train strikes tomorrow.'

She sighed. 'Go on, then. I suppose it's too late for you to cancel the job?'

'I can't cancel,' I said. 'It'd be really bad for my reputation if I did. Besides, this job will give me more experience to put on the website and might gain me some new clients.'

'I don't like it,' said Charlie. He paced back and forth between the hob and the sink, alternating between keeping an eye on the bubbling sauce and me. 'I mean, I know you can only tell us so much, but from what you said earlier on the phone, you've got to pose as an instructor. You don't know anything about outdoor activities, do you?'

'A bit,' I said. 'My grandad taught me how to light fires, and make rope swings, stuff like that.'

'Yes, but that was over fifteen years ago, wasn't it?' said Daniel. 'And making a rope swing isn't exactly a survival skill is it?'

'I'll be fine,' I insisted.

'Of course you will.'

I turned at the familiar voice to see Michael leaning against the door frame, his arms folded. His eyes crinkled in amusement before he murmured his thanks to Louise as she handed him a glass of red wine.

'What do you think?' I asked.

'I think you won't find out until you do this,' he said. 'But if you cancel the job, you'll always wonder what you're capable of, won't you?'

'Exactly,' I said, wagging my finger at him. 'So, I'm booking the train tickets.'

Charlie went back to the hob with a sigh. 'Well, make it quick – I'm dishing up this in five minutes.'

I grinned, turning my attention to the laptop while Dan and Michael fetched cutlery and plates from cupboards and drawers. Louise poured more wine, and pulled up a chair beside me, twirling the stem of her glass between her fingers.

'I don't doubt you can do this,' she said. 'But will you promise me something? Let us know you're okay every day, all right? Just a text message to one of us to say that you're safe.'

I clinked my glass against hers. 'I'll do my best, but there might not be a signal where I'm going. It's an overnight camping trip, after all.'

She nodded and peered at the screen. 'Isn't there an earlier train than eleven-thirty?'

'There are two, yes.' I grimaced. 'But I don't do early mornings, you know that. This one will get me to Windermere just before four. I'll still arrive at the adventure centre in daylight so I can have a look around before I start my training on Friday.'

'I'm dishing up,' Charlie called over.

I closed the laptop and put it back in my tote bag, my thoughts already on the train journey the next day while the family's conversation turned to their weekend plans and which staff members were available to help with shifts at the fish and chip shop.

Because I intended to make that four-and-a-half-hour trip worthwhile. I was going to investigate Ethan Kingsley's background and find out why his last fiancée had disappeared without a trace.

CHAPTER NINE

I reached the platform at Euston Station the next day with fifteen minutes to spare.

It was my own fault. I'd dithered while trying to decide whether to face the Tube once more with all my kit, or take a ride share car, and by the time I decided the ride share was the more sensible option, the only car available was a small two-door hatchback with a dodgy exhaust.

The driver's eyes had widened when I appeared at the communal entrance to the block of flats I rented in, and I could already see him calculating how he was going to fit so many bags – and me – into the compact car.

In the end, we settled on putting the two heavier

bags in the back with the seats folded down, and I travelled with my backpack on my lap, peering over it to see through the windscreen and checking my phone every thirty seconds to see if we were going to make it on time.

When we arrived outside the station, I opened the door and stumbled onto the pavement and then hefted each of the other bags onto my arms. When I clanged my way through the turnstiles, almost dropping my phone while I tried to scan the booking code, I resembled an octopus with a shopping problem.

By the time I found a seat in a quieter carriage with a table to put my laptop and water bottle on, I was out of breath. Storing the two heavier canvas bags in the luggage rack near the doors, I put the backpack in the rack above my head and sat for a moment to collect my thoughts.

The train wasn't as busy as I thought it would be, and for that I was grateful. I had a protective sheet of plastic that obscured my laptop screen whenever I worked in public, but I didn't want to strike up a conversation with random strangers either.

Instead, I wanted to delve into Ethan Kingsley's background, especially now that I was going to meet his mother this weekend as well as his new fiancée.

I took a sip of water and signed into my laptop as the doors swished shut and the train eased itself from the station, heading north.

First of all, I wanted to find out more about Seamus Kingsley, Ethan's entrepreneurial father, starting with the feature that accompanied his reaching the *Times*' list of top business start-ups from four years ago.

The report summarised Seamus's achievements since he had left school at sixteen with only a handful of qualifications and a reputation for truancy. That reputation changed when he began working in a distribution warehouse for a large supermarket chain. His ability to analyse and process inefficiencies within a twenty-year-established system brought him to the attention of senior management, and his swift climb through the ranks to a place on the executive team by the time he reached twenty-four was legendary within the industry.

Not one to rest on his laurels, Seamus spent the next ten years leading takeover bids for rival stores, leaving his management role in his mid-thirties and going on to create two online start-ups that he financed with his own savings.

One of those start-ups was sold to a competitor for

an undisclosed amount of money six years later, although the rumours at the time suggested it was at the higher end of seven figures. The other start-up was the business that catapulted him to being a national figurehead of British business, culminating in the award four years ago.

The photos that accompanied the feature showed Seamus as a young boy in school uniform, an early posed management photograph from his supermarket distribution days, and one of him and Isabella at a formal function to raise money for a charity a few years ago. The remaining photograph was one taken especially for the feature and showed Seamus, Isabella and their two adult children at the Kingsleys' home in Surrey.

Ethan Kingsley was a good-looking man, with his mother's pale skin and his father's height. In the photograph, he wore his brown hair tied back in a ponytail and wore a black shirt with blue jeans. His sister stood beside him, a few inches shorter and with dark hair worn in a similar style to her mother's. Seamus stood at the back of the group, his arms around his wife's and Ethan's shoulders while he beamed at his daughter.

The caption below the image stated that both children were highly successful in their own right, with Ethan managing a consultancy, and his sister Emily running an online boutique clothing shop.

The feature ended by speculating that Seamus Kingsley's next lifetime achievement would be a knighthood.

Flipping heck.

I looked up from my laptop to see lush green countryside zipping past the window, and blinked. I hadn't realised that we had already left London behind. The train shot past the platform at Kings Langley and powered northwards past Hemel Hempstead, the hours and minutes ahead of me diminishing.

I turned my attention to Ethan. I'd already completed a brief search after leaving the Zervases' house last night that covered his social media profiles (three, two unused for nearly four years and one professional networking site) and a website for his business that provided a biography for its creator alongside three of his executive management team.

At thirty-two years old, he was a rising star according to the media, and a photogenic one at that. He had lost the ponytail from the earlier photograph taken with his family and now wore his brown hair in a shorter style. Piercing green eyes peered out from every image, his jaw set in a determined expression that accentuated high cheekbones and a nose that might have been broken once.

The most recent article I found online about Ethan was a short interview given last year with a well-known men's magazine. Scrolling through the text, I found out that he was determined to expand the business globally, kept fit by mountain biking, trail running and rock climbing, and that breakfast was his favourite meal of the day (there was a picture of him with a large plate of food, and my stomach rumbled).

The last question from the interviewer was whether Ethan saw himself as his father's natural successor, whereupon he replied, "I'm nothing like my father". Despite his words, I could sense the competitiveness emanating off the screen.

Next, I searched for his name on a business registry website. There, I found details about his business, the latest balance sheets (healthy), and a list of minor changes to the day-to-day running of the company's financial affairs. Next, I delved into his previous interests – Ethan had dabbled in a few different businesses before the consultancy took off, namely an advertising agency specialising in social media (dissolved by the director himself six years ago) and what appeared to be a financial services company that was put into voluntary administration four years ago.

I frowned.

Patricia Berriminster had said that Ethan's previous fiancée, Helen, had disappeared four years ago, hadn't she?

I clicked on the tab that named the people associated with the (now defunct) financial services business – and there she was.

Helen Dumois (resigned).

The entry was dated four years ago and the supporting documentation uploaded to the site shared only basic and formal details, nothing to help me work out why the twenty-six-year-old had disappeared from public view.

I tried all the usual social media apps next but the closest profile I found was a Hélène Dumois who lived in Aix-en-Provence, France with a pink rinse through her silver hair and bejewelled fingers who looked like she was in her eighties.

Going back to the search engine, I typed in the name of the dissolved financial services company and groaned as several sponsored advertisements appeared at the top before a list of unrelated content appeared.

I closed the laptop in disgust and looked out the window, flummoxed.

Because until I could find out the truth about Helen Dumois and why she had disappeared before her wedding day, I was at a loss as to how I was meant to protect Natasha Berriminster.

CHAPTER TEN

It was raining by the time the train pulled into Windermere station.

After a near-disaster while I was changing trains at Oxenholme that resulted in my almost missing that stop due to one of my bags snagging on a mountain bike that was stored next to the doors, I was weary of travelling and hungry as well.

At the end of the Lakes Line, Windermere station was the final destination for millions of visitors every year, but today I was the only one who looked as if I was there for the scenery. A man in a suit hurried from the train with his phone to his ear the moment the doors swished open, and a woman wearing a long cream raincoat and black trousers at the far end of the carriage gave me a surreptitious look before scurrying from the train.

I hoisted my backpack over my shoulders, pulled my bags from the rack, and almost tumbled onto the platform with the weight before righting myself and giving the station manager a weak smile.

'First time here?' he said, opening the accessible exit gate for me.

'Yes,' I replied, sidling through the metal turnstile and huffing under my breath as it spat me out the other side. 'How can you tell?'

'You all start out with loads of gear,' he grinned. 'Next time, I reckon you'll only bring that backpack.'

'You're assuming there'll be a next time,' I retorted, and stomped my way to the exit.

There was no sign of Christopher Weller, the man who was reportedly going to meet me, and so I pulled my phone from my jeans pocket and called Patricia Berriminster.

Her number went straight to voicemail, and I glared at the screen before disconnecting. I had a feeling she knew more than she had told me about the disappearance of Helen Dumois, and I wanted some answers before Natasha and her friends turned up.

The rain was growing in intensity, so I moved under the station's eaves, flattened my back against

MURDER IN THE LAKES

the wall to avoid the worst of the squall, and made my next phone call.

Shaun Hendrick was a detective sergeant with Thames Valley Police who I had met during my first forays into private investigation. I'd uncovered some distressing details about a client's future spouse and after discussing the matter with her, she had urged me to contact the police. The wedding was called off, and the ex-fiancé was now serving a three-year prison sentence at His Majesty's pleasure somewhere in Essex.

After that, Hendrick had become a valuable ally. Although I was under a code of conduct when it came to client confidentiality, I also had to follow the same rules as the police, and he was always on hand to provide advice whenever I needed it.

He answered after the second ring. 'Harper. What are you up to now?'

'I'm in the Lake District, keeping an eye on a client's daughter.'

'You don't usually go out in the field.' He paused, and I could hear the rustle of a crisp packet. 'What's changed?'

'The groom's last fiancée disappeared before the wedding,' I said. 'And I was wondering if you'd be able to do a little digging for me. I can't find much online.'

I heard Hendrick's chair creak as he sat upright. 'Give me the details, and I'll take a look.'

'Thanks.' I rattled off Helen's name and what scant information I had gleaned so far. 'I'm meant to be posing as an activities centre guide to keep an eye on the new fiancée while I'm looking into the groom's background. I haven't found anything so far to suggest foul play, but I'm keeping my options open.'

I glanced up as a dark grey rugged four-by-four turned into the station car park and drove towards me. 'My ride's here. Hopefully they've got mobile phone coverage where I'm going, so I'll check my messages whenever I can, and the same with email.'

'Leave it with me,' said Hendrick. 'I'll be in touch if I find out anything.'

'Thanks. Lunch on me when I get back.'

'Deal.'

I ended the call as the four-by-four eased to a standstill beside me and pocketed my phone while the driver peered at me through the windscreen, his jaw set.

He didn't move until I hefted my bags towards the

back of the vehicle and put them inside but then climbed out and glowered at me. 'Melody?'

'That's me,' I said, thrusting out my hand. 'Christopher, isn't it?'

'Chris. Chris Weller.' He shook my hand briefly, the scowl remaining. 'Just so you know, I think this is a bad idea.'

'I thought you might. So, now we've got that out of the way, how are we going to make this work?'

CHAPTER ELEVEN

The drive to the activities centre took forty minutes, the first twenty-one of those passing in silence while Chris brooded over the steering wheel and zigzagged his way out of Windermere and towards the activities centre at Tarrant's Cross.

Lush woodland and rolling hillsides surrounded the lanes as we climbed steadily away from the lakeside town, and I twisted in my seat to marvel at the weakening sunlight catching the water's surface. Here and there, I could see boats of varying sizes making their way back to shore before darkness claimed the landscape, some heading over the lake to smaller villages that clung to its fringes.

The four-by-four smelled of old coffee, oil and damp dogs. I had spotted pale hairs clinging to the worn upholstery in the back, together with an old horse bridle fashioned into a makeshift lead coiled next to the spare wheel, but there was no sign of the dog.

There was a bump, the vehicle jolted, and then the noise of the engine shifted, its low purr changing to a growl as the incline increased and my ears popped. I squeezed my nose and blew out, equalising them before turning my attention to the road.

Except there wasn't a road anymore. Chris had turned onto a narrow winding dirt track that twisted and turned its way up a steep slope, the right-hand side of which was fenced off with barbed wire. The left-hand side was a sheer drop only separated from the track by a narrow verge of scrubby grasses, and I felt my mouth dry as I surveyed the main road below. The tyres slid out from under us, and I hissed through my teeth before Chris slipped the gears into four-wheel-drive mode and the vehicle straightened. A sheep raised its head from beyond the fence as we drove past, a look of astonishment on its face before it resumed grazing.

I eased my fingernails from the armrest set into the door and tried to relax. Chris evidently knew the route well – he was expertly manoeuvring the four-by-four between potholes the size of moon craters without slowing down – and the sun was casting a warm glow across scurrying clouds that framed the hills in every direction, creating some of the most beautiful scenery I had ever seen.

'Have you been to the Lakes before?' he said over the noise of the uneven track, breaking the silence between us.

'No, and I'm wondering why,' I replied. 'I've just never had the chance, I suppose.'

'What do you know about outdoor bushcraft? Patricia didn't say much on the phone.'

'I'll bet.' I shifted in my seat to face him, adjusting the seatbelt so it didn't dig into my shoulder. 'I've never done anything like this before. I spent time running around the woods when I was a kid, but I'm going to be relying on you and your colleagues to teach me as much as you can to get me through this weekend. Sorry.'

He acknowledged the comment with a curt nod. 'I thought as much. I couldn't find out much about you online, but I got the impression you were more comfortable in urban environments, not out here.'

'I won't argue with you there.' I paused while he slowed to negotiate a hairpin bend in the track that crooked its way around to the right and up an even steeper slope. 'How do you propose we do this then?'

'As simply as possible.' He rubbed a hand over a jaw that was covered in days-old stubble. 'I was speaking to Ava and Noah about it earlier this afternoon, and we've got some ideas.'

'Ava and Noah?'

'They're the two guides who'll be taking the hen party group out this weekend. Ava's been with the company for the past three years after moving from Northumberland, and Noah's my brother. We started the company together nine years ago. Ava was in the emergency services before joining us, and she's led expeditions in India and Nepal. Noah and I both love the water and mountains equally, so it made sense for us to base ourselves here.'

'What sort of ideas do you have in mind?' I said, anxiety tuning my voice up a notch. I cleared my throat. 'I mean, obviously I'll be deferring to them, right?'

'Hang on.' Chris slowed the vehicle as a five-bar metal gate came into view, blocking the track.

I heard the wind howl when he got out, and it buffeted the four-by-four, rocking it from side to side. The light was fading now, fast, but I could just make out the faint glimmer of the final vestiges of sunlight on the lake far below us and shivered.

He swung the gate open, then climbed in and

edged the vehicle forward before stopping again. ''Scuse me.'

I twisted in my seat as he extracted a padlock and chain from the glove compartment.

'Back in a sec,' he said, and disappeared once more.

While he secured the gate behind us, I nibbled at a fingernail that was already ragged. The temperature had dropped considerably since we had left Windermere station behind, and I was beginning to wonder if my clothing choices were sufficient. In the shop yesterday, Will and Lynn had seemed to know what they were talking about, but we were in London, and I'd never thought to ask them about their outdoors experience, had I? To me, I was just another customer – and they might have been earning commissions on any sales, so…

The driver's door was wrenched open, and Chris clambered in, his hair windswept and a sprinkling of rain across his jacket's shoulders. He shoved the four-by-four into gear and powered it onwards before speaking again.

'We keep the gate locked at night to stop anyone accidentally stumbling down some of the crevices that are around here. We're lucky in that we've got a couple of small potholing locations on the site, but the best ones are over the way in Yorkshire.'

I swallowed. 'Do people often fall down them?'

'Only once.'

I frowned, then looked across at him to see a smile teasing at the corner of his mouth. 'Very funny.'

'It was mostly sheep that got into trouble,' he said with a small shrug, the smile fading, 'so our insurance required us to make the place secure and we can't afford the premiums to go up. It's expensive enough as it is. Plus, the farmer who owns the flock we just drove past got fed up having to retrieve the bodies.'

'Oh.' I fell silent as the track kinked to the right and we plunged into a wooded area that enveloped the vehicle and blocked out the remnant light.

Autumnal leaves still clung to branches in places, but the thick birch and oak trunks prevented me from seeing further than a few metres into the undergrowth, and the longer twigs smacked against the paintwork and windscreen. The track deteriorated further, and Chris steered along two deep ruts that were waterlogged in places, lurching forwards while he rode the clutch to avoid getting bogged.

I shivered. 'So... about those ideas. What have you got in mind?'

In response, he pointed to a string of yellowing

lights in the distance that flickered as the boughs above us shook and creaked in the wind. 'We're here. Why don't I introduce you to the others, and then we'll tell you over dinner?'

My stomach rumbled in response. 'Sounds good to me.'

CHAPTER TWELVE

Chris rolled the four-by-four to a standstill outside a sprawling lodge constructed from red brick and timber. It was a single-storey building that extended to the left and right of a central entrance, which was sheltered from the elements by a second slate-covered pitched roof and large oak doors. A tall brick chimney protruded from the middle of the roof, and the sweet aroma of woodsmoke filled the air.

One of the doors had been pulled open and a woman in her early thirties stood at the threshold, her frame silhouetted by the light from inside. She wore a thick cream-coloured woollen sweater and grey walking trousers, with her feet ensconced in scuffed canvas lace-ups. She eyed me warily as I got out of the four-by-four, her arms folded across her stomach while she cradled a coffee mug in one hand, turning her attention to Chris when he called to her.

'This is Ava,' he said. 'Ava, meet Melody.'

'Hi,' I said, thrusting out my hand. 'Thanks for putting me up at short notice. Or putting up with me, at least.'

She didn't smile, and held my hand a little too long, squeezing it. Resisting the urge to roll my eyes – or execute a quick non-lethal karate manoeuvre that would have had her sitting on her backside within seconds – I relaxed my hand such that she had to let go. 'Nice to meet you.'

Ava peered past me. 'You're late. I've made up the spare room at the back of the staff quarters. She can have that. Noah's dishing up dinner in fifteen minutes.'

'Okay.' Chris opened the back of the vehicle as she moved back into the house and pointed to my bags. 'Let's get these to your room, and then you can sort yourself out after dinner.'

'Right.' I heaved my backpack over one shoulder, lifted one of the sports bags with the other and cast a sideways glance at Chris. 'Any chance you could bring that one for me?'

He picked it up with an ill-disguised sigh. 'When

you're out here, you're responsible for carrying your own equipment. Don't forget that.'

'Once I find out what I'll actually be needing "out here", I'll bear that in mind,' I said, keeping a light smile on my lips. 'And thanks. Lead on.'

He slammed the door, locked the vehicle and stalked into the lodge, using his booted toe to shut the front door after I'd stumbled over the threshold. 'Boots off here. House rules.'

I looked to where he pointed and saw a rack containing two pairs of worn walking boots and stooped to unlace mine while he toed off his, then followed him through a reception area passing a second inner doorway, and gasped.

I paused for a moment, taken aback by the enormous space. A log fire burned off to the right of the room, with three long sofas grouped around it in a rough C-shape. A rug had been placed in front of the sofas, and a large wooden coffee table stood on top of that. A shelf under the tabletop contained old board games and some scuffed paperbacks that were several years old. Towards the back of the room there was a bookcase lined with computer games, more books, and several old, pink-covered Ordnance Survey maps folded up and stacked in a haphazard pile. The left side of the room was taken up by what looked like the old mahogany bar from a typical English pub, except there were no beer pumps or other paraphernalia. LED spotlights in the ceiling had been strategically placed to enhance the relaxed ambience in the room rather than detract from it, and two floor lamps lit up the darker corners.

'Wow,' I managed.

'It used to be a smallholding owned by a couple in their seventies,' Chris said. 'Noah and I bought it from them when they retired and moved into a place down in the valley.'

'Did you do all this yourselves?'

'With a few friends helping, yes. Come on, this way.' He walked past the room and over to an open doorway in the left-hand corner of the reception area, pointing to another door as we walked along a short passageway. 'The staff accommodation's along here. Natasha and her friends will be staying in the rooms on the right-hand side of the property. The dining room's through that door, behind the reception room, and the kitchen's off that. There are toilets off the entranceway, and en suites in the rooms.'

'Okay.' My head swivelled this way and that as he spoke. 'Anyone else staying here this weekend?'

'No, just the hen party. There's five of them, plus

you now. That's enough this time of year. This is yours.'

He opened a door and flicked a light switch, revealing a plain room with a small, double-glazed window that was being buffeted by the wind, and a narrow bed against one wall. There was a pine wardrobe that had seen better days, and a matching bedside cabinet. Chris dumped my bag onto the bed, returned to the door and jerked his thumb over his shoulder. 'Reckon you can find your way back to the kitchen in five minutes?'

'Yes, no problem.'

'See you in a bit, then.'

He closed the door, and I dropped my holdall to the floor before letting the backpack slide off my shoulder to join it, biting back my trepidation.

Like it or not, I was here.

And there was no going back now.

CHAPTER THIRTEEN

By the time I worked my way back to the door to the kitchen, voices emanated from the room, two men and a woman bantering about the food, the choice of music that was playing in the background, and the new visitor.

There was laughter following a murmured comment that I didn't quite catch, and I exhaled, then squared my shoulders. I rapped my knuckles twice against the open door before walking in, fixing a smile to my face. 'That smells good.'

Three faces turned to me, the woman's face turning stony.

'Found us okay, then?' said Chris.

'Bodes well for any orienteering over the weekend,' I quipped. I gestured to the paraphernalia covering the kitchen worktops. 'Can I help with anything?'

'Not on your first night here,' a second man said. He was slightly shorter than Chris, with shaggy dirt-blond hair and green eyes and wore a navy polo sweatshirt over blue jeans. Stepping closer, he thrust out his hand. 'I'm Noah. You've already met Ava, haven't you?'

I turned to the woman in time to see her eyes narrow.

'Just so you know—' she began.

'Yes, I do. None of you want me here,' I finished. 'Shall we get down to business? My client's daughter is turning up in less than twenty-four hours, and we've got some work to do before she gets here.'

Ava's mouth dropped open, but then Noah elbowed past her with plates and a handful of cutlery. He plonked the lot on a pine table in the middle of the kitchen and returned to the hob.

'Let's eat while we talk,' he said. 'Otherwise, this is going to spoil, which would be a shame because we don't get the chance to have fresh venison that often.'

'Venison?' I managed.

'The neighbouring landowner has to cull a few every now and again,' Chris explained. 'Otherwise, the herd will starve.'

'Which means us locals get free meals,' said Ava. 'And we get to eat this before the paying guests turn up.'

Noah brought over the enormous pot he'd been stirring and set it on a cork mat in the middle of the table before handing me the ladle. 'Visitors first.'

'Thanks,' I said. I spooned some of the delicious-smelling stew onto my plate and sat across from Ava while she and the others helped themselves.

The talking stopped for a few minutes while each of us savoured the rich flavours. It was delicious and warming. As the conversation resumed amongst the three activity guides, I sat and listened, absorbing the atmosphere and feeling my shoulders relax for the first time since Tuesday.

'So, the ideas we have for this weekend,' said Chris, setting down his fork and folding his arms on the table. 'We're working on the basis, like Patricia advised on the phone, that you have no previous experience doing anything like this before, even as a paying guest, right?'

'Right,' I conceded. Suddenly I wasn't hungry anymore, and after pushing the last mouthfuls of stew around my plate for a few more seconds, I gave up and put down my knife and fork. 'What are you suggesting we do then?'

'What we don't want to do is end up having to babysit you as well as the hen party when they turn up,' said Ava. She turned to Noah and Chris. 'I've said it before, and I've got no problem saying this again in front of Melody. This is a bad idea.'

'Of course it is,' I said cheerfully. 'But here we are.'

Chris waved his hand for silence. 'Here we are indeed. I was reviewing the activities that Natasha Berriminster and her party are interested in – obviously they're only here for two days so they're not going to be able to do everything they selected, but we have to give them their money's worth. You've got to appreciate, Melody, that we run quite an exclusive operation here. The client pays, and the client gets what they want – within reason. Usually, we only stop them from doing something if safety requires it, for example if the weather changes at the last minute, or something like that.'

'Patricia Berriminster said they wanted to do hiking, archery and clay pigeon shooting, so I can't see any of that being a problem,' I said, then saw Chris cast a sideways glance at Noah while Ava guffawed before covering her mouth. 'What?'

'Did she mention the climbing, abseiling and

outdoor survival skills?' said Noah. 'Because that was at the top of their list.'

'And those are the activities we've planned for them,' Chris added. 'Along with the usual overnight camp on Saturday.'

'Patricia never mentioned that,' I squeaked, then cleared my throat. 'I mean, I'd assumed there'd be a camping element, but… what outdoor survival skills?'

'We'll be taking them – and you – on an overnight hike with as little equipment as possible,' said Noah. 'So tomorrow we'll need to teach you how to make a shelter from whatever you can find, start a fire and keep it going, and run through some basic first aid, just in case.'

'The overnight survival skills activity is one of our most popular,' said Ava. 'People want to know that if they get stranded somewhere out of phone range or whatever that they could wait for rescue for a few days. Noah will show them how to catch and kill their own dinner as well.'

Her eyes gleamed, and I felt my stomach plummet.

'Oh,' I managed.

Noah took pity on me then. 'You won't have to do that if you don't want to. It's an option, that's all.'

'What's the other option? Go hungry?' I said.

That at least caused a smattering of polite laughter, but when I looked at Chris, his face was without humour.

'Better go get some rest while we clear this away,' he said. 'It's going to be a long day tomorrow, and we'll be meeting in here at eight to begin your training.'

'Right, okay.' I rose from the table and took my plate over to the sink before turning to the three of them. 'Thanks again.'

Their murmured voices were left in my wake as I hurried from the room, dismissed.

When I reached the bedroom that had been allocated to me, I closed the door and leaned against it for a moment. The walls were bare brick, but the room was warm, so I guessed there was insulation behind those even if Chris and Noah hadn't bothered painting them. The wooden floorboards were exposed, sanded down and accompanied by a pair of threadbare rugs. It was clean and functional but nothing more.

I moved to the bed, removed my thick socks and massaged my feet. Will and Lynn at the camping shop had told me my walking boots would take time to get used to, and I could feel the start of a blister on my left heel. Rummaging around in my bags, I found my little first aid kit and slapped a plaster over the skin before brushing my teeth.

Picking up my phone, I checked it for any messages or missed calls. There weren't any, and as I lay back against the pillows and started scrolling through that day's news cycle, I bit back the temptation to call Patricia Berriminster and tell her I'd changed my mind.

Because I knew then that I was completely out of my depth.

How was I meant to protect Patricia's daughter if I couldn't look after myself by the end of tomorrow's training day?

CHAPTER FOURTEEN

At seven the next morning I was showered, dressed, and in the kitchen before anybody else.

The kettle had finished boiling five minutes ago, and I now stood at one of the windows overlooking the rolling landscape beyond the activities centre's perimeter fence.

A fine dew clung to the windscreen of Chris's four-by-four, and in the weak pale glow of an autumnal sunrise I could see mist rising from the bottom of the hillsides, and a lone deer silhouetted against a backdrop of gorse and grass. Opposite the kitchen window were two Land Rovers parked next to each other outside a locked corrugated iron barn, both dark grey and both bearing the centre's logo along the sides. A solitary hatchback, battered and light blue, was parked behind those, and I wondered if it belonged to Ava or Noah.

The Aga in the kitchen was still warm from the previous night and I sidled closer to it as the enormity of what I was doing sank in. Pretending to be one of them, hoping Natasha's future mother-in-law wouldn't latch on to who I was or what I was up to, and trying to protect the bride-to-be from any threats weighed on my conscience. I'd never been a good liar, and so I hoped Chris and the others would be able to teach me enough today, so I'd at least be useful to them while looking out for Natasha.

I blew out my cheeks. I'd find out soon enough, but in the meantime I could make sure all of us were ready for whatever the day was going to throw at us.

Putting down my coffee mug on the table, I started to explore the cupboards and refrigerators, and soon I had the beginnings of a cooked breakfast on the hob.

Noah appeared just before eight o'clock, his eyes lighting up when he saw the sausages frying in the pan. 'I thought I could smell food. How long have you been up?'

'Only about an hour,' I said, stirring a pan of mushrooms that I'd laced with a little garlic. 'I figured we'd all need some fuel before making a start this morning.'

'Sleep well?'

'Sort of. I'm not used to going to bed that early.'

'It takes some getting used to,' he said, pulling plates from a cupboard and cutlery from a drawer. After setting them in the middle of the table, he walked over to the kettle and plucked three more mugs from a selection on the draining board. 'You'll be shattered later today, what with all the fresh air and learning new skills. We have the guest lounge through there, but to be honest it's rare that it gets used after the first night.'

Ava appeared then, and my stomach twisted. Dressed in a well-worn parka and walking trousers, she exuded confidence as she strode across to the back door and stuffed her feet into a pair of walking boots on the coir mat.

'I'm just going to check the guns,' she said. 'One of them needed oiling, and I'm due to do a stock check on ammunition.'

With that, she disappeared through the back door, her blonde hair billowing around her as the wind tried to find its way into the warmth of the kitchen.

I shivered. 'I might put a base layer on before we head outside.'

'You'll need it,' said Noah cheerfully. 'The weather up here can change without warning. Wear layers that you can strip off if you need to. It's much easier to cool down than it is to warm up.'

'Got it.' I glanced over my shoulder as Chris entered the kitchen. 'Breakfast? There're sausages, mushrooms and scrambled eggs. Well, they were going to be fried, but they had other ideas, so scrambled it is.'

He peered into the pan, then nodded. 'Okay, thanks.'

I dished up three platefuls, put some sausages and mushrooms to one side for Ava, and wolfed down the lot while I listened to Chris and Noah discussing the morning's plans.

'Have you ever used a shotgun?' said Chris.

'No,' I replied, setting down my knife and fork before taking a slurp of coffee. 'I've used a pistol before at a gun club demonstration day, but nothing else.'

'What about any bushcraft, such as making your own shelter or starting a fire?'

'No.' I saw him shoot a sideways glance at Noah. 'But you'll be doing that, won't you? I thought I'd just be helping to carry stuff, run errands, that sort of thing.'

'Better if you know how,' said Noah. 'Just in case one of the guests asks you.'

'Maybe it'd be better if we just tell them she's a trainee.'

I twisted in my seat to see Ava standing on the threshold, her grey eyes steely. I hadn't heard her return and watched as she set down a box of ammunition on the table, the cartridges inside clattering together.

'Maybe,' I said.

'Trainee or not, you're still going to be expected to know the basics,' Chris insisted. 'Natasha and her friends will, and it'll do no good for your cover story if they know more than you, will it?'

'True, and we can't afford for her to make us look like idiots,' said Ava, tossing a set of keys to Noah before turning to me once more. 'We get a lot of our business through recommendations, and if they don't enjoy themselves this weekend it could affect our sales.'

I stood then and collected the three plates. 'There's food over on the hob if you want some. I'm ready when you are.'

Noah pushed back his chair. 'I'll see you outside in ten minutes. We'll start by going through the equipment we'll be using this weekend so you can get familiar with that.'

'Sounds good, thanks.'

'Make sure you pay attention to what he tells you,' said Ava. 'Some of that equipment is dangerous, and we don't want any injuries, do we?'

I forced a smile, despite the chill that chased down my spine at her words. 'No, we don't.'

CHAPTER FIFTEEN

I staggered when I walked out the back door, battered by a strong wind that tugged at my clothes and whipped my hair into my eyes.

It howled around the back of the accommodation block, sent an empty black plastic rubbish bag tumbling across the yard between the activities centre and the barn, and tore the yellowing leaves from a large oak tree next to Chris's four-by-four.

Shivering, I put on the woollen beanie hat I'd remembered to tuck into my pocket before leaving my room, and made sure it covered my ears. I looked beyond the perimeter fence to the hills beyond and saw that a fine drizzle was giving the landscape a thorough soaking.

Noah seemed unaffected by the weather and

whistled under his breath while he strode across the cobbled yard ahead of me, jangling a set of keys in his hand.

The barn was several years old with its corrugated iron panels rusting in places, but in the dwindling light of the previous afternoon, I had failed to spot the new padlock fitted to an equally robust door set into the far side. The large double doors in the middle of the structure were closed, and I noticed an identical padlock on the latch for those.

Noah slowed and turned to me as we drew near. 'There are two sets of keys for this, both kept in the safe in Chris's room. We didn't have room in the house for an office or anything when we renovated it, so we keep all the paperwork and stuff in here too.'

I looked around at the surrounding countryside. There were no other houses or farms within sight, and only one car driving along a road at the top of the highest ridge. 'Do you get a lot of break-ins around here?'

'Some farmers had machinery stolen about five years ago,' Noah explained as he removed the padlock and shoved it into his pocket. 'But we have the gun cabinet in here as well, and we're required to secure that by law. We'd lose our licence for the clay pigeon shooting otherwise.'

I nodded. I was familiar with the government regulations regarding any sort of gun – including air rifles and those in historical collections – and followed him through the door. 'How many shotguns do you have?'

'Six in total, but we only allow four out at any one time. That way, we've got two spares in case one of the others can't be used for whatever reason. Besides, our policy is to only have four people shooting at any one time, no matter the size of the group. It's easier to keep an eye on everyone that way.' Noah paused to reach through the darkened doorway and find the light switch. It flicked on to reveal a concrete floor laced with oil and tyre marks near the double doors, and a sectioned-off area in the left corner. 'That's the secure room we use as an office, and the gun cabinet's kept in there.'

I followed him across the barn, craning my neck to see the steel roof rafters and seeing the remnant stains from pigeons. I could hear them cooing somewhere and realised we had startled them into hiding when Noah had rattled the padlock. The corrugated roof was dry on the inside, without any of the damp patches I expected to see, and the walls looked as if they had been retro insulated to keep out the chill and prevent any water ingress.

And it worked. Despite the wind rattling the outer shell, the inside of the barn was much warmer.

On the right-hand side of the barn, I passed steel shelving units that were organised by activity. Here, there were colourful ropes looped into tidy piles, over there were tents packed away in polyester covers, and I spotted at least four camping stoves poking out from a metal box at the far end.

None of this interested Noah. He made a beeline for the secure room, typed a six-digit code into the security panel to the right of the door and swung it open.

'Ava's our firearms expert, although Chris and I will run the clay pigeon shooting from time to time,' he said. 'That's why she was out here earlier. She does a stock take before and after every booking, and then a random one now and again to make sure nothing's been taken without us recording it.'

I ran my hand down the side of the door, noticing the bright brass locking mechanisms. 'I can't imagine anyone's going to break in here without you knowing about it though, are they?'

'Hope not. Here, give me a hand.' He walked over to a large steel cabinet that resembled a narrow wardrobe and tapped in the six-digit code again, the musical notes resonating off the bare walls. Swinging open the door, he stepped aside so I could see. 'There are a number of disciplines in clay pigeon shooting, but we limit ours to skeet so we only have semi-automatic shotguns. They're lighter and have a lower recoil so they're perfect as an all-round offering for our clients.'

I eyed the gleaming guns lined up side by side. 'Aren't semi-automatics dangerous?'

'These aren't like pistols or assault rifles,' he explained. 'These limit a user to three cartridges, which they need to fire by pulling the trigger each time.'

'And where are the cartridges kept?'

'Separately, in that safe over there.' He jabbed his thumb over his shoulder to a bulky rectangular lump of metal that was set into the floor beside two filing cabinets. 'And we're limited by law about how many we can stock of those as well. Here, take this.'

He handed me one of the shotguns, and I tested its weight in my hand. It was well balanced, and not as heavy as I'd imagined. I stepped out of the way as he slammed shut the door and locked it, then moved over to the safe and removed a box of cartridges.

'These contain lead alloy pellets that will shatter the birds when they hit them.'

'Birds?'

'It's what we call the targets. Live pigeon shooting was banned back in 1921 but a lot of the old terminology is still used in the sport.' Noah waved me to the open door of the storeroom, then locked that behind us. 'Those and the trap – the machine that projects the birds into the air for us to shoot – are already out at the shooting range.'

I watched how he cradled the shotgun in his arm and mimicked his stance, keeping the interesting end of the barrel pointing downwards, and followed him from the barn and over to one of the Land Rovers. He pulled open the back door and lifted the lid of a stainless-steel box, placing the shotguns inside before locking it.

'More safety?'

'Always,' he said. 'We don't take any chances around here, not with the public being involved. We never know who's going to turn up – some are complete beginners with no idea how dangerous these things are, and others are more experienced who think they know everything.'

I smiled. 'Which one's worse?'

'Both have their challenges,' Noah said, without humour. 'Hop in. It's only a five-minute drive from here. Let's see what your gun handling and firing skills are like, shall we?'

CHAPTER SIXTEEN

In a word, I was rubbish.

I could have blamed the crosswind that streaked across the disused field that was home to the clay pigeon shooting range, I could have blamed the fact I was nervous with so much depending on me being able to learn new skills in a short space of time, but...

'Are you actually aiming for the bird, or for those trees a mile away?' Noah demanded, walking towards me while rummaging for three more cartridges from the box in his hand. 'These aren't cheap, you know, and we've only got so many to hand out tomorrow. We usually only give twenty-five to each participant.'

'Sorry.' I sighed. 'I thought this would be easier.'

I had made nine attempts to hit the target so far, but each time the saucer shape sailed into the air before dropping like a stone a hundred metres away, intact.

'At least we're saving money on those,' said Noah, following my line of sight. 'But you're not going to convince anybody that you're an expert at this.'

'Maybe the climbing and abseiling will be my forte,' I replied, snatching the cartridges from him and reloading the shotgun the way he'd shown me.

'Maybe.' He shot me a sideways glance. 'Your gun handling skills are good, I'll give you that. The main thing to keep an eye out for tomorrow is to make sure nobody loads one of these until they're here, standing at this shooting line. You'd be amazed how many idiots turn up and then start waving live weapons around while they're talking.'

'Okay.'

'Right, want to give this another go?' He took three paces back. 'In your own time. And remember to breathe.'

I nodded, tried to let my shoulders relax, and took aim.

The range was what Noah referred to as a down-the-line arrangement, with five shooting positions facing the range. I was standing in position one, nearest to the trap that flung the targets into the air.

Tomorrow, I could be further along the line – and further along from the trap, making it more difficult to give the impression I was at least adequate at the sport.

'Pull,' I yelled.

Noah activated the trap, and the next clay target shot into the air. It arced above me at a forty-five-degree angle, and I tried to remember everything he had told me in the hour we had been out here so far. I breathed out, then pulled the trigger, feeling the slightest recoil as the shotgun butt met my shoulder.

The target exploded, sending a shower of pitch and chalk across the field like a powdery firework.

I think my mouth dropped open, before I turned to Noah, grinning. 'I did it.'

'Indeed,' came the wry reply. 'Now move along to stand two and see if you can do it again.'

Any confidence I'd gained from smashing the previous target into smithereens soon dissolved after my first shot from a different position. I managed to hit it after three attempts, which – let's face it – was an improvement on the first, but by the time I reached stand number five, there was only one cartridge left in the box and there were more untouched targets scattered on the ground than obliterated ones.

Noah checked the time on his phone as I loaded

the shotgun. 'We're going to have to wrap this up – Ava needs to head into town, and she wants to run through the bushcraft training with you first, and then Chris needs to show you some basic abseiling skills before Natasha's lot get here.'

'Let me have one last go?' I pleaded.

He seemed to think about it for a moment, then gave a slight shrug. 'Go on then.'

I watched while he walked back to the trap and settled into an old battered tartan-patterned deckchair beside it, ready to release the spring mechanism.

I wasn't perfect, and I wasn't sure whether I could be convincing as a staff member at the activities centre yet either but despite everything, I had to admit I was enjoying myself. There was a satisfaction in hitting a fast-moving target whilst trying to account for wind speed and direction, my heart rate, and any distant noise distractions.

I would have to remember all of that and act as Noah's second-in-command tomorrow when Natasha's hen party took to the range, and the responsibility was starting to weigh on my conscience. I was all too aware of the firepower in the weapon I held, and how dangerous it could be.

If Patricia Berriminster was right, and Natasha's life was in danger, the shooting range would be a golden opportunity for something to go tragically wrong and be labelled an accident rather than murder.

I blinked, swallowed, and then called out. 'Pull.'

The trap clattered, the target shot upwards into the grey sky, and I breathed out, waiting.

The moment it started to fall, I pulled the trigger.

And missed.

I saw Noah's shoulders sag, and then I breached the shotgun, kept the barrel aiming at the ground and walked over to where he waited by the trap. 'It was worth a shot.'

He raised an eyebrow in response. 'I'm glad you think so, because your next job is to go and pick up all the birds you missed.'

CHAPTER SEVENTEEN

Ava glared at the four-by-four when Noah drove me into the wooded glade where the bushcraft training would take place.

Her expression was sullen under a woollen hat that had bobbled with age and then she shoved her hands into her jacket pockets when I climbed out. Thankfully, she aimed her displeasure at Noah.

'You're late. I've only got an hour before I'm meant to be driving over to Hawkshead.'

'I thought you were just going into Windermere?' he said.

'They've run out of what I need.' Her eyes flickered to me. 'How did the clay shoot go?'

'I…'

'She did all right, considering she's never handled

a shotgun before,' said Noah, interrupting me. 'I don't think we'll have much to worry about this weekend.'

Ava didn't look convinced but gave a shrug. 'Fine. Right, let's see how you get on with building a shelter and getting a fire going, shall we?'

With that, she turned her back and walked away, following a mud-strewn path through the undergrowth before disappearing out of sight.

I glanced at Noah. 'Thanks.'

'She can be... difficult sometimes, that's all. It's nothing personal,' he said, then pointed in the direction Ava had walked. 'The bushcraft hut is through there. We have a lot of kids out here during the summer months, Scouts, Girl Guides, that sort of thing, so we built a rough shelter to use while we do the health and safety briefings when it's wet. You can't miss it.'

'You're leaving?'

'Chris and I need to finish making up the guest rooms and prepping for dinner and everything while Ava's teaching you.' He gestured to the second four-by-four parked under an enormous ash tree. 'Ava will take you over to where we do our climbing activities after that so you can go through the basics of abseiling with Chris.'

'Okay. See you later.'

Squaring my shoulders, I spun on my heel and hurried along the uneven path. I could see Ava's boot prints in the mud, but no one else had passed this way since it had last rained three days ago. I crossed my fingers and hoped it would remain that way over the weekend. I had no inclination to sleep in a tent – or a cobbled-together shelter – while the heavens opened above me and delivered a drenching.

The shelter was further along the path than I'd anticipated, and as spiky shrubs and tall grasses slapped against my legs and grasped at my arms, I started to wonder whether Ava had simply disappeared, leaving me to find my own way back. I strained my ears but couldn't hear her four-by-four starting up.

And then I burst through the trees into a leaf and pine needle-covered glade, the weak pale light breaking through the branches above and casting shadows beyond a central fire pit lined with uneven stones. I spotted the shelter in the far-right corner. Its sides were made from long branches leaning against each other with ropes at the top to hold them in place, and smaller branches had been woven between, creating a screen between the inside and the elements. The roof had been laid with much the same material with pine branches over the top. Here and there, moss was starting to grow, and if I hadn't have known what to look for, I might have walked straight past it.

Ava sat cross-legged at the entrance, wielding a vicious-looking knife while she whittled a length of wood. 'Didn't get lost then?'

'That would've taken some doing,' I replied. 'There's only one way in and one way out.'

'Oh, there are a few ways to find this place, if you know how. I guess you just didn't see them.' She flipped the knife shut before walking over to the fire pit and handing me the length of wood. 'Have you ever lit a fire this way before?'

I eyed the sharpened end of the stick. 'I haven't, but I've seen it done.'

'That's not the same. It's harder than you think, you know,' she said imperiously. 'So, pay attention.'

It took all of my resolve, but I resisted the urge to throw a mock salute and instead reminded myself that Patricia Berriminster was paying me a good sum of money to be here. So, I nodded mutely and squatted beside Ava next to the fire pit while she showed me how to gather leaf litter and small twigs before choosing one to drive the longer stick into. She then twisted it between her hands, her palms travelling from the top of the sharpened stick to the bottom.

Suddenly a wisp of smoke floated upwards from the assembled dried leaves, and I gasped.

Ava snorted. 'Didn't you think it would work?'

'Not so quickly, no.'

'Well, I have done this a few hundred times.' She leaned closer, then threw a handful of dirt over the smoke, obliterating it. 'All right, your turn.'

I took the stick from her, shuffled closer and eyed where she had placed it before. I could still see scorched twigs, so I placed the stick beside those and started twisting it.

Five minutes later, there was still no trace of smoke, let alone a roaring fire.

'The timing's imperative out here,' Ava scolded. 'The longer you take to do this, the colder you're going to get. And hungrier. And our clients aren't going to be impressed if they can't eat after a day's hike.'

'I think the wind's stopping it.'

'No, it isn't. I've done this in the rain,' she boasted. 'You're just not doing it right. Watch.'

She snatched the stick from me, placed it a little way over into a fresh pile of leaf litter, and I swear she had that fire going in thirty seconds.

'Try again,' she said, standing and kicking some dirt over the fire once more. 'Over there.'

I looked to where she pointed and saw a tiny pile of leaves and twigs in the far corner of the pit. 'Hang on.'

Walking over to the far side of the clearing, I hunted around until I found some more dried leaves that were sticking out from an old fallen tree trunk and had missed that week's rain. I added those to the small pile in the pit, made sure there was plenty of space between them to let air get in, and started twisting the fire stick in my hands.

I had blisters by the time I saw smoke, but I let out a whoop that echoed off the surrounding trees. I sat back on my ankles, grinning.

'Well, don't just sit there – you need to feed it some more fuel, otherwise it's going to go out,' Ava snapped. 'Use some of those bigger twigs and build it up without stifling the air flow.'

Despite wanting to push her face into the nearest muddy puddle, I did as I was told and soon a sizeable fire was burning in the pit. 'What sort of things will we be cooking on this over the weekend?'

'We'll take basic supplies such as a water filtration pack, noodles, some homemade cereal bars packed with carbohydrates and protein – lightweight things that don't weigh us down – just in case we don't catch anything for dinner tomorrow night.'

'Catch?' I watched as she made sure the fire was extinguished. 'What are you hoping to catch?'

She shrugged. 'Probably fish. We've got a licence for the local waterways so we can feed our clients. If I'm out on my own, I'll set traps for rabbits, but I can't do that with clients. They tend to get a bit squeamish.'

I shivered. 'Can't think why.'

Ava shot me a sideways look, then tilted her head towards the shelter. 'Let's see if you can build a smaller one of those, shall we? Otherwise, you might not have a roof over your head tomorrow night. I'm not sharing mine.'

CHAPTER EIGHTEEN

Let it be known that I'm not too bad at building an overnight shelter, despite anything Ava might have said to the others later that day.

I quite enjoyed the process, if I were honest. There was something satisfying about weaving in the longer branches amongst the pole-like ones I'd used as my basic structure, and given I was only meant to build one big enough to house one or two people, I chose to make it lower to the ground than Ava's, thereby keeping it out of the wind a little more.

Standing back and watching with her hands on her hips while I crawled inside and checked it for comfort, she watched me with impatience.

'Right, that's enough,' she said. 'I need to get to Hawkshead by two o'clock.'

'What's in Hawkshead?'

'None of your business.'

She was already walking towards the path out of the woods by the time I crawled from my shelter, and I hurried after her. 'Thanks for taking the time to show me all of that. I appreciate it.'

Ava spun around, a snarl on her face, and jabbed her forefinger at me. 'I'm only showing you because I have to. As far as I'm concerned, having you here this weekend is a risk. You've got no experience with any of this, and yet here you are. So do me a favour and just do as you're told. We don't need to try and be friends, all right?'

With that, she strode away, leaving me standing in the middle of the path on my own, stunned.

Then I narrowed my eyes at her retreating figure.

I was no stranger to a challenge, but if I had to work my backside off this weekend to escape Ava's wrath, I would do so – and keep Natasha Berriminster safe.

Then I heard a shout.

'If you want a lift instead of walking back to the activities centre, you'd better get a move on.'

I could take a hint.

I ran.

The drive back to the activities centre passed by in silence, and the moment I climbed out of the four-by-four on the fringes of a field a few hundred metres away from the driveway entrance, Ava hit the accelerator, churning up mud as she powered towards the track that led down the hill.

'What's wrong with her?' asked Chris, walking over from his own vehicle with two harnesses slung over his shoulder and a large canvas bag in his hand.

'Apparently I made her late for an appointment in Hawkshead,' I said.

'Hawkshead?' He frowned, watching her four-wheel drive as it disappeared over the brow between two gorse bushes. 'I thought she was just going to Windermere?'

'She told Noah they didn't have what she wanted in stock.'

'Oh.' He didn't look convinced but handed one of the harnesses to me. 'Okay, well here you go. Climbing one-oh-one coming up. Ready?'

'Yes.'

He must've heard the doubt in my voice because he cocked an eyebrow. 'Are you sure?'

'I'm just a bit tired, that's all. It's been a busy day. Lots to learn,' I explained. 'I'll be fine.'

'Follow me then.'

He unclipped a latch on the top of the metal five-bar gate leading into a field of mown grass and locked it behind us before setting a brisk pace towards a large metal and wooden structure over on the left-hand side.

It towered above me, and as I got closer I eyed the wooden walkways suspended high above my head, my gaze moving to a solid wall constructed from multiplex board that had different coloured blobs of polyurethane fixed to it. Some were red, some were blue, others were yellow, but they all had one thing in common – they started about half a metre from the ground and rose steadily upwards in different patterns.

My heartbeat calmed a little. 'I thought we'd be climbing real rocks.'

'We will be tomorrow. This is our training wall. We start all our beginners here,' said Chris as he dropped the canvas bag to the ground and unzipped it. 'We use this to assess everyone's comfort with heights before we run through the basics. We won't need to do that with Natasha's group – they've climbed before, although to different standards.'

I fell silent as he explained about the different ropes, knots and harness settings that would keep me safe while I scaled the wall, craning my neck at the end of the demonstration to peer up at the summit. 'It's very high.'

He laughed. 'It's only five metres. Come on, let's make a start. Remember, use your feet and legs to push your way upwards rather than pulling yourself up with your arms. You'll tire too quickly otherwise.'

'Okay.'

We spent the next two or three minutes with me scrambling for suitable hand holds and toe holds while Chris called out instructions and belayed a rope that I threaded through stainless steel anchors as I progressed. The rope – once I'd gained some height – would prevent a nasty landing if I did lose my grip.

'Stop there,' Chris said.

I looked down, then up. I was still three metres away from the summit. 'Why?'

'Let go.'

My attention snapped back to him. 'What did you say?'

'Let go. You need to know how to fall safely.'

My mouth dried, and my fingers clawed tighter at the hand holds I was gripping. 'Do I have to?'

'You can't try abseiling from the top until you do.'

I closed my eyes and sighed. 'Fine. What do I do?'

'Just push yourself a little away from the wall and let the rope do the rest. I'll control the fall, don't worry.'

And he did.

My heart was racing as I gave myself a shove away from the handholds, my feet were suddenly dangling in mid-air, and then I was falling.

Except I wasn't, because Chris was right. As he steadied my fall, a smile formed on my lips and by the time I plonked myself on the ground beside him, I was grinning.

'Okay?' he said.

'Yes.'

'Right, same again, all the way to the top. Choose your holds carefully and remember to take your time. You can abseil from the top this time. It's a few metres short of the one we'll do on the ridge tomorrow, but it'll give you some practice. Wait a minute.' Chris held up his hand to stop me as his phone started ringing and he answered it. 'Hey, what's up…? What, now?'

I watched while he checked his watch and grimaced before turning his attention back to the caller.

'I can be there in fifteen minutes. Okay, laters.'

He hung up and stuffed the phone into his jacket pocket before beckoning to me and then started unbuckling my harness. 'Natasha's party are already in Windermere. They'll be here in twenty minutes, so we have to get back ASAP. I need you to put this equipment away in the barn while I'm doing the meet and greet bit with Noah and Ava. Keep this set-up as yours – if you hang it up on the peg on the far left as you're looking at all the kit in the barn, you'll be able to use it again over the weekend.'

'Okay.' I swallowed. 'They're three hours early.'

'I know.'

'But I haven't abseiled properly yet.'

'I know.'

'And I still haven't learned how to do half the bushcraft stuff because Ava had to go out. All I've done is build a tiny shelter and light a fire.'

'I know.'

'So—'

'We'll work something out, say you're learning on the job or something, but we have to get back now. Apparently, they want to do the clay pigeon shooting today rather than Sunday afternoon while it's still light enough.' He gathered all the rope, coiling it expertly while he spoke and then placed it in the back of the four-wheel drive. 'Let's go.'

I followed mutely, climbing into the passenger seat and fastening my seatbelt a split second before the vehicle surged forward. As we bounced over wheel ruts and splashed through muddy puddles, I clung to the strap above the door while my body rocked with the motion of the off-road vehicle and my stomach lurched.

Heart racing, I went over in my mind what I'd learned that day, and it felt woefully inadequate. I had simply taken too long to learn all the new skills that were required to make this assignment a success – and keep Natasha Berriminster safe.

CHAPTER NINETEEN

My first impression of Natasha Berriminster was that I was in trouble.

She stepped out of a shiny black four-by-four that hadn't been off-road in its entire lifetime of approximately one year, surveyed the activities centre and the surrounding buildings with a look that suggested she had seen better, then beckoned to me, her long black hair billowing around her shoulders.

'Good afternoon,' I chirped. 'Welcome to the Weller Adventure Centre. Did you have a good journey?'

'It was fine, thank you,' she said, then glanced over her shoulder as a woman with a brunette bob approached. 'Hurry up, Sarah, otherwise I'm claiming the best bedroom for me.'

Sarah looked at me as if I was something she had trodden in.

'Fetch the bags, will you?' she said, before beckoning to two others who climbed out of the vehicle and were giggling. 'Come on, let's see what the rooms are like. Don't expect too much, these places are usually very basic.'

With that, she slipped an arm around one of them, with darker hair who I recognised as Ethan's younger sister Emily, and laughed as the other, a willowy blonde, managed to side-step a pile of rabbit droppings at the last minute.

'Gosh, you'd have thought they'd have cleaned the place before we got here,' she grumbled as the four guests wandered towards the centre's entrance.

'Gosh, you'd have thought you'd expect to see bunny poo in the countryside,' I muttered, crossing to the four-by-four and heaving the bags from the back of it. I don't know what this lot were planning on this weekend, but the bags were heavy, and I staggered under the weight of them.

'Oh, good. That's a relief.'

I looked over my shoulder to see a woman in her fifties standing beside the second black four-by-four, the tailgate of which was open. She had her dark blonde hair scraped back in a no-nonsense ponytail and wore grey cargo trousers and a dark green fleece. Craning my neck to see past her, I noticed that the back of her vehicle had been fitted out with different hooks and netting that accommodated various outdoor equipment. Climbing ropes, kayaking paddles, life vests, ski poles – you name it, it was there, all in its own designated spot. A wire mesh separated the back from the passenger seats, and this had been kitted out with a fabric shelving unit that looked as if it contained a whole heap of other paraphernalia, ready for the outdoors or whatever other adventure she was pursuing.

So, this was Isabella Kingsley.

'Would you like your bags taken in as well?' I ventured, my arm muscles already protesting in anticipation.

'Not at all,' she said, turning and hoisting an enormous backpack onto her shoulders before reaching in and picking up a large sports bag. 'I simply wasn't prepared to carry all of theirs as well.'

She breezed past me with her bags as if they were lightweight pillows and called ahead to Natasha and the others. 'Make sure you take your boots off at the door, girls. It's good manners.'

A chorus of giggles followed her remark, but I didn't hear the response – I was too busy trying to work out which bag belonged to who from the jumble that now lay at my feet.

'Here.'

I looked up to see Noah advancing towards me. 'Eh?'

'I'll give you a hand. Ava got back early so she's showing them where to find their rooms, and Chris is sorting out the paperwork for them to sign. Waivers and stuff.'

'Oh. Okay. Thanks.'

'After we've done this, I'll need to head back to the kitchen while you and Chris take them clay pigeon shooting.'

'Me?' I gulped. 'Are you sure there isn't something else I could help with?

'Not right now, so you might as well make yourself useful. Dinner won't be ready for another couple of hours – I haven't finished prepping the meat yet, and it'll take a while to cook. I tend to run the kitchen and the small bar we've got in the visitor lounge.' He shouldered four of the bags and waited while I slammed shut the tail gate. 'I have a feeling this lot are going to be thirsty later on.'

'I can look after the bar for you later if you need a break,' I said, following him into the activities centre.

MURDER IN THE LAKES

'I worked in a pub while I was at university. If you want me to, that is.'

'It'd certainly help. All you need to do is write down what they have, and we'll add it to their bill when they check out.'

'Easy.' I shifted the remaining bags on my shoulders. 'Right, lead the way.'

I hadn't seen the guest wing yet and took the opportunity to have a look around while we delivered the respective bags to the rooms.

Natasha's room, the best one according to Noah's murmured commentary, was the furthest from the middle of the building. It afforded a modicum of quiet from the busy entrance and guest lounge area, as well as avoiding the noise and smells from the kitchen when that was in use. I groaned as I dropped her bags just inside the door.

Having her placed so far away from me was going to make it difficult to keep an eye on her.

'Do you have security cameras around here?' I asked Noah as he reappeared from what would be one of the bridesmaid's rooms.

He shook his head. 'Only above the reception door, and two out in the yard facing the gate in case anyone shows up while we're not around. Chris probably told you about the insurance company requirements.'

'Yes.' I paused and looked back along the corridor to the other doors. 'So, we've got Sarah next door here, then Grace, the blonde, and then Emily, Ethan's sister, and finally Isabella, all the way down the end next to the dining room.'

'Her idea,' Noah said as we walked back towards the reception area. 'She reckons after a day out in the fresh air, she can sleep through anything, and I reckon she's stayed in worse places than this and loved every minute.'

I smiled. 'I got that impression too.'

CHAPTER TWENTY

It came as no surprise to me that Natasha was well versed in the use of shotguns.

From what Patricia Berriminster had told me, and from my own research, it seemed that Ethan Kingsley's future wife was one of those people who could turn their hand to anything involving outdoor sports and adventure.

The rest of the hen party were of varying skill levels, and I kept a wary eye on them, mindful of all the things that could go wrong. They listened with impatient expressions while Chris spent twenty minutes explaining all the health and safety rules, then eagerly followed us to the barn and paced beside the large open doors while we fetched the guns and ammunition.

We walked to the target area rather than split the group into separate vehicles, and as Chris led us along a meandering route through a wooden five-bar gate and alongside a drystone wall covered with patches of moss, I inhaled the fresh cool air and marvelled at the breathtaking scenery around me.

It was apparent from the start that a competitive streak existed between the friends. Their laughter carried along the line to where I helped Chris load the trap before he released the targets into the air, whilst Isabella coached her daughter in the finer techniques of the sport at the far end. Emily cast a wistful glance every now and again at the ease with which her future sister-in-law was hitting the clays but then refocused and fired at the targets she was assigned.

Despite the overcast sky, the wind dropped after an hour, and the targets exploded with more regularity, so much so that without telling the women, Chris adjusted the trajectory to make it harder for them. He saw me watching and gave me a wink.

'Don't worry, they'll enjoy the challenge, and we save some money on buying new birds,' he said. 'At the end of the day, we're running a business here. I can't afford to give these away.'

'That makes sense.' I shielded my eyes and watched as Sarah, the brunette, fired the next round and missed, her shoulders sagging with disappointment while Grace's target shattered as it found its arc. 'She's good.'

'She's patient. See how Sarah doesn't wait until the clay starts to fall? That's where she's going wrong.' He paused with his hand on the trigger and waited until the last shot had been fired before calling over. 'We're heading back in thirty minutes, ladies. Make the most of it.'

Natasha raised her hand in response, and the others sighted their shotguns once more, waiting for Chris to recommence firing the targets, and I stood back as another fusillade of exploding cartridges filled the air.

By the time it was four o'clock, the clouds were parting on the horizon, revealing a soft ochre sun that was starting to dip towards the hills at a rapid rate. It would be dark within an hour or so, and after checking that all of the shotguns had been made safe and all the unused ammunition was accounted for, Chris guided the group back to the activities centre along a different route that followed a bubbling brook.

We paused on an ancient stone bridge to admire the sunset through the trees, and I had to admit, it was breathtaking. I didn't see sunsets like this in London, not with all the buildings cluttering the skyline and for a moment I let myself relax and enjoy the view.

When we reached the yard fifteen minutes later, Chris handed three shotguns to me while he took the rest from Isabella and pointed the group towards the house. 'Dinner will be served in the kitchen at six o'clock, so that should give you time to freshen up. There's plenty of hot water, and you'll find towels and hairdryers in your rooms. If there's something you need that we've overlooked, please just ask. Make yourselves at home, and we'll see you in a while.'

There were murmured thanks as they removed their boots and disappeared inside, and then I followed Chris back to the barn.

'That seemed to go okay,' I said as I watched him set each of the shotguns on a bench beside the cabinet before cleaning them.

'It helped that they'd all done it before,' he agreed. 'And starting them off with something like that after such a long drive helps them let off some steam and get some fresh air at the same time. They'll be able to relax tonight before tomorrow's early start. You did okay out there, too.'

I smiled. 'Thanks.'

I jumped at a scratching sound out in the main

section of the barn beyond the door, and he laughed. 'It's just the cat that hangs around here, don't worry.'

I wasn't convinced – it sounded bigger – but I fixed a smile to my face as he went back to working on the guns.

'Would you pass me that oil over there on top of the filing cabinet?' he said. 'I'll give these a quick wipe down, and you can rack them in the gun safe. The code is two, one, seven, four, seven, six.'

I did as he asked, feeling for the first time like I had achieved something this week, and more hopeful that I would be able to look after Natasha Berriminster while she enjoyed her weekend activities.

Soon, the safe room carried the sweet aroma of gun oil, and as Chris finished cleaning each shotgun, he passed it to me.

'Why did you decide to start an activities centre?' I asked while we worked. 'Had you done anything like this before?'

'No, but I've stayed in places like this, both here in the UK and overseas when I was travelling between school terms and university semesters,' he said. 'I knew about this old farmhouse from a few hikes I'd done with Noah and friends over the years so when I heard it was up for sale from one of the locals, I couldn't resist taking a look.'

'And Noah was keen as well?'

'As soon as we saw it, we knew we wanted it.' He smiled and handed me the last shotgun. 'It's been a lot of hard work, and we've had some hiccups over the years, but we're still enjoying it.'

'That shows,' I said, and I meant it.

After the shotguns were locked away I paused on the threshold of the safe room while Chris made sure the door clicked into place by pushing against it. Satisfied, he led the way through the barn, the dull ceiling lights chasing shadows into the corners and suspending dust motes in the air.

'I'll get up early to sort out these so you can be off straight after breakfast,' he said, running a hand over the coiled climbing ropes lining the shelves before ushering me out to the yard. 'The first day can always feel like a rush otherwise, what with trying to get the clients out of bed on time.'

It was dark outside now, and there was a cold nip to the air that would turn frosty within a week or so. There wasn't a cloud in sight, and I paused for a moment to look up at a myriad of stars, their celestial journeys speckled with the light from hundreds of satellites that whizzed across the night sky.

I could smell Noah's cooking carrying on the breeze from an open window in the kitchen.

'I'm starving,' I said.

'That smells delicious,' Chris agreed.

And I was, despite the trepidation that was creeping back, taunting me. Despite showing an adequate level of understanding with the clay pigeon shooting, I had still only completed a tiny amount of the training the others had planned for me, I was sure. And here I was, surrounded by people who had a hundred times more experience, and I was supposed to be protecting one of them.

'I need a hand serving dinner,' Noah said, poking his head around the doorframe while I pulled off my boots. 'You've got two minutes to freshen up, and then I'll need you in the kitchen.'

'Okay.'

As I hurried to my room, I quickly forgot about how well the shooting had gone. Instead, I felt a pang of anxiety about the other activities Natasha and her friends would be doing, and feared the rest of the weekend would be an even greater challenge than I could imagine.

CHAPTER TWENTY-ONE

Isabella might have been at home outdoors, but it was soon evident that she wasn't comfortable in social situations. Sitting at the far end of one of the large four-seater sofas in the guest lounge, she looked as if she would rather have been on a windswept mountain somewhere in Nepal than having post-dinner drinks with her future daughter-in-law and friends.

Which made me wonder why she had insisted on coming along to the hen weekend.

I watched the small group from behind the bar while I pulled out bottles from a locked cabinet underneath the stainless-steel sink and made sure the ice-making machine was fully stocked and working.

Chris had served wine with the evening meal, a hearty lamb stew cooked by Noah that was devoured by the women while they discussed the wedding. I hovered on the fringes of the group, handing out condiments and taking away dirty plates while eavesdropping on the conversation.

Emily, Ethan's sister, tried her best to fit in but it seemed to me that Natasha and her friends only tolerated her presence due to the future family aspect. She kept her phone on the table beside her wine glass and checked it from time to time, sometimes typing a rapid text before attempting to catch up with the conversation with a bemused expression.

It transpired that Grace Masters, the blonde, was going to be Natasha's maid of honour. They'd known each other since they were thirteen, and it was Grace who was with her when she met Ethan at the orienteering event in Wiltshire.

'Not that it was very difficult,' Grace recounted at the table. 'All we had to do was circumnavigate Avebury and the West Kennet long barrow. Most people just went along for the social aspect and the pub lunch afterwards.'

Isabella looked as if she was fighting off boredom by that point. 'You should do some real orienteering from time to time, here or in the Dales, or the Scottish Highlands – anywhere that's a real challenge. Where your life depends on getting your way points right.'

'Just as well we're doing this weekend, then,' said Sarah Llewellyn, the brunette, looking around at her friends. 'Because I'd be useless. I'd be the one they'd have to call out the air ambulance for, knowing me.'

That caused a ripple of laughter, and then Natasha told a story about an incident that took place five years ago, only reinforcing Sarah's penchant for clumsiness.

Now, the five women were sitting on the sofas, their murmured conversations interrupted by the occasional clatter of plates and cutlery from the kitchen while Chris and the others cleaned up and had their dinner. I'd managed to sneak away and eat some of the stew in the kitchen in between helping them, and was now sipping a can of energy drink I'd found in the back of the bar refrigerator.

After a quick slurp, I wandered over to take the first drinks order of the evening, clearing my throat as I approached. 'Would anyone like a drink? We've got beer, wine, a selection of spirits…'

'I'll have a G and T. That's a gin and tonic to you.' Sarah lifted her nose a little before turning to Natasha. 'I'd be surprised if they're even serving those here.'

I fixed her with my most dazzling smile. 'Would

you like ice and a slice with it? That's frozen water and citrus fruit to you.'

Natasha emitted a snort, before attempting to recover with a coughing fit that fooled nobody while Sarah's jaw dropped.

She looked like she'd sucked on a wasp. 'I, er... yes. Please.'

'Coming right up.' I turned away in time to see Isabella looking at me, bemused. 'Would you like anything, Mrs Kingsley?'

'Just a glass of white wine please. Dry, if you have it.'

Natasha followed me over to the bar and watched while I mixed the drinks and selected a Sauvignon Blanc from the back of the refrigerator for Isabella. She glanced over her shoulder before leaning her elbows on the countertop, lowering her voice. 'Sorry about Sarah.'

'Thanks. Did you want a drink?' I said, scooping ice into two glasses.

'A rum and coke would be good.' She gave a shy shrug. 'It's not fashionable, but I have a sweet tooth.'

I held up the can of energy drink and shook it gently from side to side. 'Me too. Go and sit down, and I'll bring over your drink.'

'Thanks.'

After delivering the drinks and leaving the women to enjoy the cosiness of the open fire that was blazing in the hearth, I retreated to the bar and found a stool to sit on while I updated my notes on my phone using an encrypted app. I had chosen to travel without my laptop, reasoning that I had enough to carry with all the clothing and equipment needed for the weekend.

First impressions were that all of the women were capable of doing the planned activities, but all of those had an element of danger that, if someone was a threat to Natasha Berriminster, would mean I'd have to be vigilant for the next forty-eight hours.

The women seemed close, and no doubt looked out for each other bearing in mind the number of tours and treks they said they had undertaken together, and Isabella seemed to get on well with Natasha given the way the two of them were laughing and talking about next week's wedding while sipping their drinks, so maybe the threat would come from an outsider – but who?

Patricia Berriminster had only engaged my services because Ethan's previous fiancée had gone missing before the wedding, and until Hendrick managed to dig up some details about what had happened to her, I was stuck chasing shadows.

'I was wondering if I could have a top up?'

I jumped and looked up to see Isabella leaning on the bar. 'Sorry. Of course, coming right up.'

'I didn't mean to startle you,' she said, holding out her empty wine glass. 'And use this – it'll save washing up two, won't it?'

'Thanks.' I tucked my phone into my pocket and crossed to the fridge, returning with the Sauvignon Blanc. 'How are you all settling in?'

'It's lovely here,' she said. 'Ethan said they'd enjoy themselves. It's why he suggested it.'

'That's your son, isn't it?' I replied, fixing an innocent smile to my face. 'Has he been here before then?'

'Once or twice.' Her face clouded as she contemplated her wine. 'Not for a few years, but he said Chris and Noah did a great job at making everyone welcome, and that the bedrooms were nicer than some places. Natasha's fine, but one or two of her friends can be... a bit picky.'

'Really?' I grinned. Given that one of the women sat near the fire was her daughter, I could easily work out who she was referring to.

She winked by way of reply, then walked back to her seat beside Emily and draped an arm around her shoulder, tuning back in to the conversations around her.

Half an hour later, the women were flagging from the long journey, the fire was a pile of glowing embers, and the glasses were empty. I wandered over to tidy up while Sarah enthused about the weekend ahead.

'We'd best get an early night.' Natasha yawned, then stretched luxuriously. 'Early start tomorrow, isn't it?'

'I can't wait,' said Grace, rubbing her hands together. 'This will be where things get interesting, won't it?'

I sighed as they teetered out of the guest lounge towards their rooms, my heart sinking.

Interesting was something I was hoping we would all avoid this weekend.

Because interesting inevitably meant trouble.

CHAPTER TWENTY-TWO

At half past one in the morning, I was still scrolling on my phone, researching.

There was an owl outside, hooting its way around the yard and no doubt keeping a wary eye on the fox that had screeched ten minutes ago, nearly giving me a heart attack.

It was raining again, and I could hear the fat splats of water splashing against the window panes in gusts as the wind caught hold. The sound made me shiver, but then the small radiator beneath the window gave a rattle and a burp, and I heard a fresh wave of hot water trickle from the pipework and wiggled my toes.

I was still cold, despite wearing my thick socks and keeping my leggings on while hugging a tepid hot water bottle to my chest while I worked.

I flicked between two different browser screens, adding to the scant knowledge I had been able to glean from cross-referencing Natasha's social media accounts with those of Grace and Sarah. The encryption software was fast and enabled me to work on a draft document saved to a cloud-based server that, in time, would form the basis of my full report to Patricia Berriminster once the weekend was over and I was back in my office.

I'd listened intently to the three friends over dinner and subsequent drinks that evening, discovering that Grace had been the one to take Natasha under her wing when they ended up at the same boarding school as teenagers, and who shared her love of the outdoors.

They had gone backpacking together in their late teens, exploring Thailand and Vietnam, and were planning to continue their trips away from time to time, when Natasha and Ethan's plans allowed.

Natasha had met Sarah at a friend's party while they were both at university. They hit it off after discovering they could both belt out the same karaoke numbers without the aid of an autocue and had been inseparable ever since.

Sarah was less adventurous than Natasha and Grace, and seemed aloof compared with them, compounded by her treatment of me in the guest lounge that evening. When I started to delve into her background a little more however, I discovered that she was from a middle-class background in the south-east, and so I wondered if her attitude was simply a misguided attempt to look as tough as the other two this weekend.

My thumb worked the screen until I found one of Sarah's social media sites was still open publicly. There was nothing in the posts to worry an employer though, and she seemed to go months without updating anything. An occasional funny meme or thoughtful quote interrupted the otherwise tame selection of photographs, and she didn't appear to respond to any of the birthday messages posted to her timeline earlier that year.

I stopped, rubbed my eyes, yawning as I spotted the time displayed at the top of the phone screen and groaned. I was meant to be awake in less than four hours, and I still hadn't finished updating my notes.

Then I blinked as I found the last entry on Sarah's timeline.

The final photograph was one taken of the three friends only four months ago, at Natasha and Ethan's engagement party. Grace and Sarah had looped their arms through hers, champagne glasses in hand. All three were beaming, Grace saying something to Natasha while Sarah had her head thrown back, laughing.

I turned out the light after that, with my final thoughts before sleep spent wondering who on earth would want to hurt any of them, and that maybe Patricia Berriminster was wrong.

CHAPTER TWENTY-THREE

My alarm went off at the abhorrent time of half past five.

Bleary-eyed, I slapped the front of my phone to silence it and stared into the darkness for a moment, heart thumping.

When I reached out to switch on the bedside lamp, blinking as my eyes adjusted, I could just make out the sound of a robin chirping in the yard outside. Every now and again, a wind gust shoved against the window, and I shivered at the thought that I was going to spend the next two days out in the elements.

I was already looking forward to getting home tomorrow night and a hot bath.

The room was cold, and as I pulled on more layers, remembering all the advice I'd been given over the past three days about how to keep warm, I wondered again whether I should have accepted Patricia Berriminster's request for help.

Surely there were more adept people she could have employed? Ex-armed forces, for a start. There were plenty of ex-servicemen and women offering private security, so why not one of those? Unless, as she had said, Ethan Kingsley's father was so well connected that even one of those might have a conflict of interest and alert him to the fact that the mother of the bride-to-be had trust issues.

I checked my phone for missed calls. Still nothing from Shaun Hendrick, and I didn't know if I'd get a phone signal once I was out in the hills.

There was a light knock on my door, and I opened it to see Noah standing in the hallway wearing a navy fleece, waterproof trousers and thick socks. He carried a bright red jacket with reflective strips on the front of it over his arm and carried his backpack and a woollen hat.

'Ready?'

'Yes.' And I was, despite my nerves. I was pleased to see he wore similar clothing to mine, although I had a sneaking suspicion there were fewer layers underneath his fleece, and as I shouldered my backpack and closed my bedroom door, I realised I wasn't nervous, I was excited.

I had never done anything like this before, and part of me wanted to see if I could. Despite the reasons for my being here, I would learn a lot over the next two days, and I loved learning.

Noah led the way out of the staff accommodation wing and into the kitchen where Chris stood over the hob, stirring an enormous pot of porridge.

'Get stuck in,' he said, ladling out a generous portion into a bowl and handing it to me. 'This'll keep you going. We've got half an hour until the guests are due to get up so make the most of it. This will be the last time you get to relax until we get them all back here safely.'

My stomach churned at his words, but I ate the food anyway, knowing I would need the sustenance until our next scheduled break, whenever that was.

'We'll aim for one o'clock,' Noah explained. 'But that's going to be dependent on what the weather does. These gusts aren't great for abseiling for a start, and the weather app shows rainfall from three this afternoon. We're due to leave here at seven – there's a lot of walking to do today.'

Ava appeared next, her hair tied in a low no-

nonsense ponytail. She was wearing thick jersey leggings that bulged with the base layer she wore underneath. She murmured good morning, then made a beeline for the porridge and spooned a generous amount of sugar over the top of it before sitting beside me.

'How did you get on with them last night?' she asked, keeping her voice low.

'No problems,' I said. 'They all seem to get on well, and there's a lot of experience between them, give or take a few minor mishaps in the past. I think they'll be okay this weekend.'

'So, now you're an expert?' she said, her cheeks dimpling.

'Hey,' I replied, holding up my hands. 'They know more than me, so that's got to be a good thing, right?'

She conceded the point with a nod, then went back to her porridge.

Isabella was the first to appear, looking fresh without makeup and wearing an ensemble of clothing that looked as if it had seen many miles of rugged terrain. She helped herself to coffee and porridge, sat at the far end and scrolled through her phone while Noah and Ava discussed last-minute preparations. Natasha and her friends appeared five minutes later, bleary-eyed but eager to start and as I watched the bride-to-be I knew I would do everything I could to keep her safe this weekend so she could enjoy her fairytale wedding.

Half an hour later, the group were ready, and seeing no sense in hanging around, Noah and Ava told everyone to fetch their backpacks and meet them by the front door.

I made my way out to where the walking boots were all lined up on the rack and found mine, lacing them up and hoping I'd remembered everything I would need.

My backpack rested easily on my shoulders, and by the time Natasha and her friends joined us, I was eager to get going.

Noah and Ava led us outside, a weak autumnal sunrise peeking through tumbling grey clouds that bustled across the horizon.

I could still hear the robin, its chirping coming from a drystone wall that separated the yard from the woodland beyond, and crows wheeled overhead, cawing to each other. The wind howled around the buildings, ruffling my hair, but I wasn't as cold as I'd expected.

'Okay, everyone,' said Noah, a huge smile on his face as we formed a rough circle. 'Are you ready?'

'Yes!'

I looked around as Natasha, Emily, Sarah and Grace chorused, and saw Isabella standing beside Ava, her expression one of concern. Ava was wearing a smile that didn't quite meet her eyes, but Noah seemed oblivious to the pair of them and instead raised his arm to beckon the group forward.

'Then, let's go!' he yelled, to cheers and whoops.

My phone started ringing right then, and when I looked down and saw the name displayed on the screen, my heart lurched.

Noah and Ava were already walking towards the gate, the hen party following at their heels, and Chris was standing on the threshold of the lodge, arms crossed while he watched them go.

'I've got to take this,' I called out to Noah. 'I'll catch up.'

I waited until I was a few metres away from Chris, made sure I still had a signal, then answered.

'Just in time,' said Shaun Hendrick. 'Thought that was going to voicemail.'

'We're going to have to make this quick,' I replied. 'We're leaving right now.'

'I'm not so sure that's a good idea,' he said, and it was then that I heard the worry in his voice.

'Why? What's wrong?'

'I did some phoning around after we spoke, and

one of my colleagues in Yorkshire Police came back to me half an hour ago with some information about Helen Dumois. It's not good.'

My stomach twisted, and I took a few steps to the left to get a better angle of sight down the muddy track leading away from the activities centre. The small group were already leaving it to climb over a stile that led through the woods and up the first of many hills, and I was all too aware that I was meant to be there with them, keeping a close watch on Natasha. 'What have you found out?'

'She's not missing, she's dead.'

'What? How?'

'The coroner's inquest said her death was accidental,' Hendrick said, 'but that was after a lot of debate.'

'Debate?'

'There were conflicting accounts about how she died. One witness said she wasn't taking enough care and was ignoring instructions she was being given – that might've led to a death by misadventure ruling – and the other said she was an experienced sportswoman who was using someone else's equipment that might not have been up to current standards. Then the insurers and the lawyers got involved, and proved there was nothing wrong with the equipment or the instruction she received, so the coroner registered the accidental death.'

I paced back and forth while I listened, then froze as I watched the last figure disappearing from sight over the stile and into the woods. 'Shaun, where exactly did Helen Dumois die?'

'She was taking part in an outdoor adventure weekend,' he said. 'At Tarrant's Cross.'

'Here?' I blurted, then glanced over my shoulder to see that Chris was leaning against the doorframe, watching me with interest, a frown on his face. I gave him a thumbs-up and a fake smile, then turned back to my phone, lowering my voice. 'They never said anything to me.'

'Makes you wonder why, given that they know you're there to keep your client's daughter safe.' Hendrick paused for a moment, and then he sighed. 'Do me a favour? Phone me or send a text tonight and tomorrow to let me know you're safe.'

'There might not be a signal out there.' My heart was racing now, trying to remember if Chris or Noah or Ava had said anything to me that warranted suspicion.

'In that case, Harper, I suggest you watch your back.'

CHAPTER TWENTY-FOUR

I found the group with little trouble, catching up with them halfway along the footpath that led away from the main track.

The woodland grew thicker here, with oak and beech boughs clustered together forming a canopy that blocked most of the weak morning light from penetrating the route Noah and Ava were taking. Enormous ferns filled much of the undergrowth, with the tree trunks covered in lichen and moss. There was a damp smell all around me, rotting vegetation vying with the drying fringes of mud around the huge puddles I stepped over.

Noah was leading the way and setting a brisk pace, closely followed by Emily and Sarah. Natasha followed in their wake, her gait easy as she laughed as

Sarah ducked under a low branch at the last minute. Behind her were Ava and Isabella, deep in conversation, voices lowered. Grace was at the rear, stopping every now and again to take a selfie on her phone or a photo of whatever caught her interest.

I fell into step beside her with a smile and willed my racing heart to slow down while my thoughts tumbled over one another.

Up ahead, Natasha had started walking backwards to talk with Isabella, her enthusiasm for the hike tinged with a wish that her future husband was here to share it, upon which Ethan's mother gave a polite laugh and told her to make the most of the weekend with her friends.

'You two are going to be so busy once you're married, it'll probably be months before you get a chance to enjoy a honeymoon,' she said.

'Oh, no.' Natasha tittered. 'I'm not waiting until the New Year. There's a new place in Grenada that's just opened up for guests – very exclusive, or so one of my clients was telling me. I've already told Ethan we're going away for three weeks next month, even if it kills me.'

A chill crossed my shoulders at her words, and I watched while she turned and quickened her pace to join Sarah and Emily.

'Have you and Natasha always enjoyed outdoor activities?' I asked Grace when she paused to prepare to jump over a brackish stream that was running across the path. Sunlight caught the water a little further along, and even I had to admit how pretty it looked.

'Pretty much,' Grace said after leaping across in front of me, her pace quickening to close the gap between us and her friends – or escape having to speak with me.

She didn't elaborate, and so I tried a different angle.

'What's Ethan like, her fiancé?'

That elicited a shrug. 'All right, I suppose. A bit older than her, but the moment she saw him at the event in Wiltshire and found out who he was, she was smitten. He's a qualified sailor and has his own yacht in the Mediterranean. We went there over the summer for a week or so.'

'All of you?'

'Not Isabella. Just us girls.'

'And you all get on with Emily by the look of it.'

'She's very easy going, just like her brother.'

The footpath grew steeper after that, and I fell silent so I could concentrate on my breathing and getting used to the strain on my knees and calves.

We popped out the other side of the woodland into a gorse-strewn hillside littered with rocks and rough grass, and the wind whipped around us with gusts that made me hunker into my jacket and pull up the collar.

I was at the rear now, with Grace catching up to Natasha and the others, and while huffing my way up an incline that was more painful than the setting on the treadmill at my local gym, I wondered if Natasha's fiancé could really be as perfect as everybody thought.

CHAPTER TWENTY-FIVE

By the time we reached the exposed crag where the abseiling activity was meant to be taking place, the wind had changed direction and clouds were scuttling across a darkening sky.

I opened my backpack and handed out protein bars to the hen party to accompany their pre-packed sandwiches and walked across to where Noah and Ava were talking, their voices low.

It looked like they were arguing.

'Everything okay?' I said as I approached, earning a glare from Ava. 'I thought I'd serve the coffee while you two are busy.'

'Thanks,' said Noah, relief evident in his voice as he pulled a large flask from his bag. 'Everyone happy over there?'

'They seem to be,' I replied, taking the coffee from him and resisting the urge to tip the whole lot down my throat. Even with the lid on, it smelled divine. 'So, what's going on?'

'Ava wants to cancel the abseiling, so we'll stop here rather than following the path that takes us around and up to the top,' he said. 'We can still climb here, but she reckons it's too risky in these gusts.'

'It is,' she insisted. 'With them climbing, we've got more control.'

'It makes no difference,' Noah argued. 'Most of them have experienced worse weather than this.'

'But not all of them, right?' I said. 'Emily for one, I'll bet. Probably Sarah too from what I was hearing last night. And they say she's accident-prone.'

'More like she won't listen to what she's told,' Ava snapped. 'And if this morning's hike was anything to go by, her reputation is correct. Did you see her nearly slip off the path when we came around the ridge?'

I had, and my heart had been in my mouth, but somehow Sarah had found her footing at the last minute and laughed it off. 'For what it's worth and given my client's insistence that I'm here to look out for her daughter's safety, I'm inclined to agree with Ava.'

She looked at Noah. 'That's a valid point.'

'Well, who tells them, then?' he said, jerking his chin towards the group of women.

Then they both looked at me.

I sighed and waggled the flask in my hand. 'Good job I can soften the news with this, isn't it?'

Four expectant faces turned towards me as I walked back to Natasha and her friends, and even Sarah looked impressed.

'Is that... is that coffee?'

'Tarrant Cross's best,' I announced, uncapping the flask, letting the delicious aroma waft on the wind towards them. 'And my suggestion? Make the most of it, because Noah didn't bring another one of these. It's a pre-climbing treat.'

'Climbing?' Natasha looked at Grace, and then me. 'We're meant to be abseiling.'

'It's too windy,' said Isabella, holding out a tin mug while I filled it, steam rising from the contents. 'I was hoping they'd make that decision.'

'But...' said Emily.

'It's a good decision,' Isabella insisted, then looked at me. 'And I'm sure it's one our hosts haven't taken lightly.'

'Noah and Ava have a lot of experience between them leading expeditions in tougher terrains than this.

If they say it's too windy for abseiling, then it's too windy for abseiling,' I said. I filled each of the group's camping mugs. 'Does anyone want sugar? I've got some in my bag.'

Natasha smiled. 'Really? Yes, please.'

I handed out the fish and chip shop-branded sachets to bemused looks, then craned my neck to look at the crag we were now meant to be climbing. 'So, what do you think?'

Isabella followed my gaze. 'It's a good choice for beginners to intermediate climbers. Nothing very taxing, but it looks like there are one or two technical parts. It shouldn't take us too long.'

'Who's taking the backpacks up there?' said Sarah.

'You are.' Noah's shadow fell over me, and I looked up to see him squinting up at the top of the climb. 'Ava will go first to act as a guide at the top of the climb, and I'll belay for each of you. Melody and I will climb last so we can bring up the spare ropes with us. The extra weight will be a challenge for some of you, but it's more realistic. You'll be able to use these skills on future trips that way.'

I felt a prickle of adrenaline at his words. At least I would be able to watch each of the women go ahead of me and make a mental note of where they chose their handholds and footholds.

Handing back the coffee flask to Noah, I followed him over to the base of the cliff where Ava was coiling ropes and checking harnesses in preparation for the climb. The ropes were all different colours, and she was scrolling through her phone while she worked.

She saw me watching and held it up so I could see. 'I'm checking the guests' weight against the equipment we've brought, just so we can account for any eventualities. You'll be fine, because you're using the same one you used yesterday.'

I looked up at the crag to see scrubby plants sticking out from crevices here and there, their stunted twigs rattling in the wind. 'What about gusts?'

'Noah and I will be able to control any buffeting the guests encounter to some extent, but it's going to be a challenge for any of them that haven't experienced it before.' She raised an eyebrow. 'Think you can do it?'

'What, without embarrassing myself?'

'Without embarrassing us,' she corrected. 'You're representing our activities centre, remember.'

I forced a smile. 'Only one way to find out, isn't there?'

CHAPTER TWENTY-SIX

Ava climbed the crag first, of course, and made it look easy.

While I was watching her, awed, I listened to the conversation around me as Isabella, Natasha and her friends discussed Ava's technique, all of them noting what they would and wouldn't do when it came to their turns.

Noah stood beside me, belaying Ava as she made her way upwards, his strong hands flowing easily over the blue and yellow rope while he called up the occasional suggestion to her. For the most part though, he remained silent, jaw set while he watched her progress.

The wind had increased now, its direction turning so that instead of blowing against the cliff face, it howled alongside it, causing Ava to be shoved sideways in places before she corrected herself.

I glanced over my shoulder. The grey clouds that had chased us up the hillside were gathering momentum, and I could see a rain front moving steadily towards us. 'Do you think that's coming our way?'

Noah chanced a quick look before turning his attention back to the belaying. 'Yes, which is why we want to get everyone up to the ridge before it reaches us. After this, it's another six miles to where we're going to set up camp tonight, and some of the ground can be difficult in wet weather.'

'Okay.'

Ava worked steadily, using her legs to boost herself upwards before pausing to pin an anchor into a crevice and attaching a carabiner. She did this on a regular basis, clipping on to each anchor herself before moving on to select the next handhold, and creating a safer route for the rest of us to follow.

'Beginners and intermediate climbers like you can clip on to each carabiner,' said Noah under his breath. 'Experienced climbers will miss some of them out to get a more technical experience, so don't try to copy what someone like Isabella will do, all right?'

'Okay,' I murmured, my mouth dry. 'Noted.'

Ava reached the top after a solid fifteen minutes and disappeared from view for a moment. When she returned, she had removed her harness and threw down a red rope that uncoiled smoothly as it fell, landing beside Noah.

'Okay,' he said, turning to the hen party. 'Who wants to go first?'

'I will,' said Isabella. 'I've managed top ropes before, so I can help Ava.'

'Fine by me.' Natasha gave her a gentle shove forward and smiled. 'I've only climbed once or twice so I want to watch everybody else before I do it.'

'Sounds good.' Noah double-checked Isabella's harness before she did the same for his belay system and then gave her a nod. 'All right, in your own time remember.'

'Thanks.'

By the time Emily, Sarah and Grace had ascended the crag, I'd managed to work out the route I wanted to take when it was my turn. The ones who had completed the climb had removed their backpacks and were milling around at the top of the ridge, sometimes hanging on to a spare rope and peering over the edge to see who was coming up next before retreating to safety from the wind.

At the top, Ava stood beside Sarah who was

holding her phone and taking pictures. Ava shooed her away, then waved her arm to signal she was ready for the next climber.

Noah turned to Natasha, holding out the belay rope. 'You're next.'

She looked up from her phone, which she had been staring at for the past ten minutes. 'Melody can go instead of me. I need to deal with this email. I'm such an idiot – I forgot before we left.'

'Are you sure?' I looked up at the cliff face. Ava was waiting, one hand on her hip but the others were nowhere to be seen. 'I can wait.'

'No, that's okay.' Her smile was strained. 'I've got a problem with the florist who's organising the wedding bouquets that I need to sort out, so you might as well.'

'Have you got a phone signal?' I said, surprised.

'No, but I'm hoping that if I hit "send", it'll go as soon as there's any chance of one.'

I held up crossed fingers. 'Good luck.'

Noah looked over his shoulder at the advancing storm front, then to me. 'Right, Melody, let's get on with it.'

I stepped forward, mentally repeating the mnemonic about the rabbit that emerged from its hole and went around the tree while I knotted the rope into my harness and then carried out the cross-checks with Noah before facing the cliff and craning my neck.

Ava seemed a long way away at that point, and I exhaled.

'You can do this,' Noah murmured while Natasha stabbed at her phone screen with her thumbs. 'Just clip into each anchor point when you reach it, take your time thinking about where you're going to place your hands next, and push with your legs. Don't rush.'

'Says the man watching the rain,' I replied. 'Okay, here goes.'

I reached up for the first handhold, feeling the cold harsh granite, and tested my weight against it.

It didn't move.

'Pick one a bit lower,' said Noah. 'Don't overstretch yourself. That's a surefire way of tiring yourself out.'

'Got it.' I felt around until I found a handhold I liked, then did the same with the first toehold.

Remembering to push with my foot rather than pull with my hand, I found the first anchor point just two metres from the ground and clipped in.

'That's it,' said Noah, flexing the rope. 'Now just rinse and repeat, all the way to the top.'

I was five metres up the cliff before I knew it, my

confidence growing each time I found another anchor point and clipped in before finding the next handhold. I took a moment then to look over my shoulder and admire the landscape beneath me, marvelling at the rolling hills that we had hiked across, and seeing another lake glistening in the distance.

Then I heard an ominous creak.

My attention snapped back to the ropes, then my harness.

There was nothing wrong there.

Then there was another grinding sound to my left, and when my eyes found what was causing it, my heart rate plummeted.

The steel anchor was loose, unable to take my weight any longer.

I gasped, frantically searching for something to hold on to.

I was too late.

My eyes widened as the anchor slipped from the rock, and then I was falling, my hands flailing at the scrubby plants, loose stones, anything to break my descent.

I couldn't.

My shoulder crashed into the granite surface, and I cried out in pain before I twisted in the air and bounced off a sharp outcrop. I moved my head at the last minute, narrowly avoiding another black eye – or worse – before plunging past the next anchor point.

Then I felt Noah take the strain on the belay.

My arm smacked against the rock wall, but I didn't notice. I was too busy scrambling for something to hold onto, trying to slow my descent before—

Too late.

I heard a grunt, a yelp of pain, and then Noah and I tumbled to the ground.

I lay looking at the sky for a moment, blinked as fat raindrops started to hit my eyelids, and then saw Ava looking down at us, her face pale and her mouth open in an "o" of shock.

Natasha ran over to us, her phone forgotten, her voice breathless. 'Are you okay?'

'I think so,' I managed, fighting down the urge to be sick. I looked sideways at the sound of a groan from Noah.

'I think my ankle's busted,' he said.

CHAPTER TWENTY-SEVEN

By the time I'd helped Noah into a sitting position and brought over his backpack for him to lean against, Isabella had steadied the top rope while Ava abseiled back down the crag to join us.

'What happened?' she demanded.

'Melody lost her grip and fell,' said Noah, grimacing while he ran his hands down his ankle.

There were no protruding bones, but it was already swelling up, and I was sure the bruises were going to be spectacular the next day.

'I didn't lose my grip, the anchor came loose,' I insisted. 'I saw it happen after I clipped into the carabiner.'

'That's impossible,' said Ava.

'Keep your voices down.' Noah shot a sideways

glance over to where Natasha was pacing the stony grass while the women at the top of the cliff stared down at us, wondering what was going on. 'There's no need to alarm the clients. Right now, we have to work out what to do next, because I'm not going to be able to climb like this, and we've already told them it's too windy to abseil.'

'I'm not happy about splitting up the party,' said Ava. 'It'll be safer to keep them all together now that we're compromised. Anyway, it's Natasha's hen weekend after all, and it's not going to be much fun for her stuck down here with you two. I think we abseil, get them all back together again, and then come up with a new plan.'

I swallowed, looking at the storm clouds.

They were tumbling towards us at an alarming rate now, gathering strength, and I'm sure I heard a rumble of thunder amongst them.

Noah followed my gaze, then turned back to Ava. 'Okay, do it. Melody and I can help from this end.'

'We can?' I squeaked.

'It's just a case of keeping the ropes steady, just like I did for you,' he said. 'I'll be there to guide you, but without putting any weight on this foot, I'm not going to be much use.'

'We'll need to put together a makeshift stretcher

for you when I get back down here,' said Ava. 'You're going to make that even worse if you try to walk on it.'

I looked over my shoulder as Natasha approached. 'Everything all right up there?'

'I think so,' she said. 'I was just wondering what we're going to do now.'

'Ava's going to bring you all back down,' said Noah. He forced a smile that didn't quite reach his eyes. 'You'll get to abseil after all.'

'Well, they will,' said Natasha, frowning. 'I haven't done anything yet.'

'Let's get everyone down here, then we'll have a chat about some different activities,' said Ava smoothly.

'How come they're going to abseil? I thought it was too windy?'

'Change of plan,' said Ava. 'The wind isn't too strong yet. It seems to have held off, so as long as we don't – pardon the pun – hang around, I should have them all down here before you know it.'

'I hope that doesn't mean they have to use Melody's technique of descending,' said Natasha. 'What if the wind picks up while they're abseiling?'

'We'll be steadying them from the top rope and

from the bottom,' said Ava. 'They might encounter a bit of turbulence, but they'll be fine.'

'The longer we talk about it, the more likely it is they'll be caught by the wind,' said Noah, his tone urgent. 'We need to get a move on.'

That galvanised everyone into action. Ava made her way back over to the cliff face, waiting for Noah and me. He hopped alongside me, arm around my shoulders to help him balance, wincing every time he had to place his foot on the ground.

'I'm sorry I landed on you,' I said.

'Me too, but the alternative wasn't going to be a good outcome for you,' he replied. 'Was it?'

My mouth dried. I was sure I was going to have nightmares for quite some time after today, and I was glad I didn't have to try to climb the crag again, but I wouldn't let it show. 'True. I don't think I'll have bounced so well.'

'Trust me, there was no bounce.'

I managed a chuckle, then sobered as we joined Ava.

'Cross-check me, Noah,' she said, looking pointedly at me.

That done, Noah showed me how to take the strain of the rope when it was needed, and then sat on the ground beside me, doubling as my belay partner and feeding the rest of the rope to me.

I watched as Ava climbed, her movements smooth and without hurry. She paused at the place where the failed anchor had slipped, and I saw her sweep her hand across the granite surface, then turned away as small stones and gravel fell.

'What's she doing?' I spluttered.

'Probably working out what went wrong,' said Noah. 'We're going to have to write up an incident report for our insurers and that'll need as much detail as possible.'

Sure enough, Ava paused, pulled her mobile from her pocket and expertly held on with one hand while she took photos with it. That done, she zipped it back into her jacket and continued her climb to the top.

When she waved, Noah held up his hand. 'Okay you can relax for a moment. It'll take a minute or two to prepare the first person to come down.'

In the end, it was Emily who abseiled first.

She landed lightly next to me, eyes wide. 'Are you okay?'

'Never better. Noah's hurt though.'

'We thought...' She shook her head. 'Never mind.'

I looked up at a shout from Ava, then raised my

hand in return. Moments later, Grace descended, giving Natasha a hug.

'We thought that was you,' she gushed. 'You have the same colour jacket.'

My heart lurched. I hadn't even thought of that, but casting my gaze over to where the two women stood talking with Emily, I realised Natasha was even wearing the same make of jacket as I'd just bought.

Was my fall really an accident, or was Patricia Berriminster right?

Was someone trying to murder Natasha?

CHAPTER TWENTY-EIGHT

It took Ava and Isabella another twenty minutes to coax Sarah into completing her descent before they walked over to where Natasha waited, nibbling her nails.

She stared at them now, ruing the fact she would have to have them redone before next weekend's wedding while I coiled ropes and watched Noah pulling a bandage from the first aid kit.

Stoical, he shot me a wan smile as I walked over to him.

'Thanks again,' I said.

'You're welcome. What happened? You were doing really well and then let go.'

'I didn't let go; I told you. The anchor slipped.'

He frowned. 'Slipped?'

'Yes, it came loose. It didn't take my weight.'

'But Ava put all of those in. She's done it hundreds of times.'

'I guess the law of averages didn't work in my favour today. And, given that it was meant to be Natasha who climbed next, that's probably a good thing—'

I fell silent as the rest of the group wandered over to join us.

Ava held up her phone. 'There's no signal, but I can radio back to the activities centre and let Chris know what's happened. Then we need to work out how to get you back.'

'That stream is about six miles from here. We should camp there tonight,' said Noah. 'We're behind schedule now, and there's not much chance of finding enough raw materials to build shelters before this rain gets heavier, so the bushcraft activities will have to wait until tomorrow – we can use the tents instead. You could go down to the woods with Melody and find some branches and stuff we can use to build a makeshift stretcher.'

'Shouldn't we go back to the activities centre?' I said.

'It's further if we turn back,' said Noah. 'It'll be dark before we get halfway, and there are potholes along that route that someone could fall into if they slip in this rain. I say we carry on to the stream. Let's face it, it's a realistic experience now, and everyone here will learn from it.'

'It's not exactly what we paid for though, is it?' said Sarah.

'Yes, it is.' Isabella shoved an empty chocolate wrapper into her backpack and licked remnant crumbs from her fingers. 'You wanted to learn some outdoor bushcraft skills this weekend. Now you are.'

'I wanted to do some fun stuff like archery, not this,' Sarah insisted, flapping her hand towards Noah.

'And we still will do that,' he said. He finished wrapping the support bandage around his ankle, then winced as he stood up. I hurried over so he could lean against me and take some of the weight off his foot. 'There's no reason why we can't set off early for the centre in the morning and be there by lunchtime. You'll have the chance to do some archery before you go home, no problem.'

'I don't know…' Natasha sighed.

Emily cleared her throat. 'Actually, I think he's right.'

We all turned to face her, and I saw Ava arch an eyebrow.

'Do you?' said Sarah.

'Well, yes.' Emily looked around at the group. 'Look, it's not ideal but as Noah said, it's going to take longer to get him back to the activities centre tonight than it would to set up camp a little further on. And it's true about learning some bushcraft skills, isn't it? I mean, I don't know how to make a stretcher – do you?'

She directed her question at Natasha, who thought for a moment, then nodded. 'Okay. But that's only if you're absolutely sure, Noah. I mean, you're the one with a busted ankle after all.'

'It's not broken,' he said with a smile, 'only badly sprained. I'm sure by the morning I'll be able to put some weight on it, and we've got painkillers I can take until then. We might even be able to do some of the bushcraft activities in the morning before heading back.'

I saw Ava looking sceptical, but she gave in. 'All right. You'll need to split the stretcher-carrying into shifts to give everyone a break. I'll stay in front when it gets dark, no matter what. The terrain around here is uneven, and there are sheer drops in places, so I don't want anyone deviating from the path I set – is that clear?'

We all nodded, and then she looked at Sarah.

MURDER IN THE LAKES

'I want you behind me. No wandering off, understand?'

Sarah gave her a dark look but murmured her agreement.

'I'll bring up the rear in between stretcher shifts,' I said. 'That way, I can make sure everyone's okay.'

'All right,' said Noah, hobbling over to his backpack and pulling out a bright wind cheater before tugging it over his head. 'It's going to be dark in less than an hour, so we need to get a move on.'

CHAPTER TWENTY-NINE

It was another half an hour before Ava and I reached the fringes of the woodland and cut two strong branches from a towering beech tree.

By then, there were a pair of tawny owls hooting from the upper boughs, and a thin sliver of moonlight blurred between the storm clouds that had gathered. Rain pelted the hood of my jacket while I trudged back to where Noah and the hen party waited, the women clustered in a separate group. They were having an animated discussion as Ava and I drew near but broke apart when Grace saw us approaching and elbowed Natasha in the ribs.

Isabella walked over, hoisting her backpack over her shoulders. 'What do you need us to do?'

'Not much at the moment,' said Ava, already pulling some nylon paracord from her bag. 'For those of you who don't know how to do this, just watch for now. I'll give you a proper lesson in the morning, but my priority is getting you to the camp site at the stream before it gets too dark. Save your questions for later, okay?'

Her tone was brusque, but nobody protested, even Sarah. Instead, we watched as one while Ava unpacked her single tent, folded it into thirds and then strapped the two branches to each side, weaving the paracord along the edges.

'Nice work,' said Isabella approvingly.

'Noah, do you want to see if you can get comfortable, and then we'll head off?' Ava asked.

I shouldered Noah's backpack while they made some minor adjustments to the stretcher, then saw Emily approaching.

'Do you want me to help you with your bag while the others are carrying Noah?' she asked.

'Thanks.'

'Okay, everyone,' called Ava. 'We're ready. On three.'

Isabella, Natasha, Sarah and Grace emitted unladylike grunts as they took Noah's weight, but once we were following Ava across the uneven ground they found a comfortable pace and were even joking with him after a while.

'I feel so guilty about this,' he protested.

'Melody's the one who should feel guilty,' said Sarah. 'She's the one who squashed you, after all.'

Jokes aside, I knew how lucky Noah and I had been. If he hadn't been there to break my fall, I might not be walking right now, if at all, and his situation might have been a lot worse too if I'd fallen any differently.

Now we formed a ragged line behind Ava, traipsing over an uneven and little-used path while the wind whipped against us, and the heavens opened. We were drenched within minutes, but despite my misgivings, my new waterproof trousers and jacket kept the worst of it from soaking through to my warmer layers. I wasn't cold – yet – but the conditions were far from ideal, and I wondered who in their right mind would choose to have their hen party in the Lake District in October.

I followed behind them with Emily in silence as my thoughts turned to the afternoon's events, and the reason for my being in the Lake District in the first place.

A few metres in front of us, Natasha was easing herself over a rugged tumble of rocks that were strewn across the path while trying to keep her corner of the stretcher stable.

I kept thinking about what might have happened if she had climbed up the crag before me, as planned. Instead, she had seen something about the wedding on her phone that had distracted her, and I'd taken her place.

Whoever had loosened the anchor hadn't planned for that, and right now I was walking alongside six people, and any one of five of them might have been responsible.

Ava had been in charge of setting the course and placing the anchors in the first place, but would she have risked doing so, knowing that Natasha was near the end of the line of climbers? Surely that anchor could have slipped from the rock face any time after she had passed, and Grace, Isabella and Emily had all ascended without incident.

I watched Sarah as she walked alongside Isabella carrying the stretcher, the two of them in Ava's wake so that the two more experienced women could make sure she didn't stumble or injure herself and Noah.

Did she loosen the anchor when she reached it?

I shook my head. Ava had been watching Sarah all the time she had been climbing, calling down instructions and, again, making sure all the climbers reached the top safely. Ava would have seen Sarah tampering with the anchor from her vantage point, wouldn't she?

What about Grace, then? She had been the one to climb before me, but I'd been watching her, anticipating her every move so that I could learn from her while listening to Noah's instructions.

My gaze fell to Emily.

She had been the first to agree with the plan not to turn back – but why? Did she prise the anchor from its place just enough that it would work its way loose by the time Sarah and Grace had passed it? Or, given that Natasha was less experienced than the others, did Sarah loosen an anchor that everybody else had ignored, because they didn't need to use it?

Or what if it was a genuine accident, and I was being paranoid?

My mind spun with all the possibilities.

In the meantime, Ava had withdrawn, her head down while she checked the route for hazards and pointed out directions for the stretcher bearers. I wondered whether that was because her plans for Natasha had failed, or whether it was from a genuine sense of guilt that the anchor had come out so easily. And what about her unplanned trip into Hawkshead yesterday? Neither Chris or Noah had known about

MURDER IN THE LAKES

that and had seemed surprised when she told them she was going.

We waded through a shallow stream, and then Ava held up her hand to bring everyone to a standstill.

'Is this where we're camping tonight?' said Sarah.

'No, there's another mile to go,' said Ava. 'We'll rest for five minutes and then swap around to give Natasha and Grace a break and carry on. We'll do the same in half a mile, so Sarah and Isabella have a rest.'

I took a moment to check the time on my phone.

It was four o'clock, and the light was fading on the horizon.

We weren't going to make it to the camp site before it got dark.

CHAPTER THIRTY

There was a wintery nip to the air as the afternoon light faded and shadows chased our heels.

Below, down in the valley, I could see tiny pinpricks of light from isolated cottages, the wind rocking trees from side to side so that the lights blinked on and off, on and off.

We had lost some altitude, and Ava led us along a narrowing path that wound its way between bracken and gorse before we delved into a thick woodland of ash, beech and oak.

I shivered as the cold breeze rattled the branches above my head, the clicking and rustling doing nothing for my heightened senses, while the rustle of leaves underfoot became a white noise broken only by the occasional twig snapping that rocketed my heart rate.

Natasha joined me after a few hundred metres into the woodland, ending her conversation with Grace and Ava to wait beside the track until I caught up. I took a moment to rummage through my backpack and extract my head torch like the others had and switched it on before falling into step beside her.

'Are you okay?' she asked. 'I'm sorry. I didn't get a chance to ask you back there.'

'I'm fine,' I replied. 'A little shaken, but all good. I feel bad about Noah though.'

And I did. He was putting on a brave face and regaling the stretcher-bearers with stories from some of the expeditions he and Chris had undertaken over the years, but we both knew how lucky we had been.

I wanted to change the subject. 'So, tell me about your future husband. Ethan, isn't it?'

'Yes.' Her cheeks dimpled. 'He's… well, he's the perfect gentleman. That sounds very old-fashioned, doesn't it? But he's so different from anyone else I've been with. Clever, kind, considerate, funny… And he loves doing this sort of thing. I mean, that's hardly a surprise given who his mother is, right?'

I looked through the gloom and torch beams to see Isabella leading the stretcher bearers, her poise immaculate, her pace unyielding. 'She's something else, isn't she? I mean, she's putting me to shame. I thought I was fit, but…'

'It's different out here to working out in a gym,' Natasha insisted. 'You're using more muscles in so many different ways. Plus, you get all this fresh air.'

At that, a particularly heavy gust threatened to shove me into a muddy puddle, and I saw the stretcher bearers hunker into their jackets. 'Oh, yes. Lots of fresh air.'

Natasha giggled. 'How long have you been a guide?'

'Not long.' I never did like lying, so I figured a little truth wouldn't be an issue, especially as I was meant to be looking out for her. 'Does it show?'

'Only sometimes. Don't worry though – I won't tell the others. What did you do before?'

'I was at university, then did some contract work here and there in offices, then took six months off to travel.' I side-stepped a rotten log covered with moss, then cast a sideways glance at Natasha. 'I started here when I came back. What about you?'

'I run my own business, selling marketing courses. I used to work in marketing for a flower wholesaler in the Netherlands after university, but I didn't like the commute and early hours.' She wrinkled her nose at the memory. 'I was spending most of my weekends travelling back and forth rather than spending time with my friends. My mother suggested I turn what I knew about marketing into a consultancy business three years ago, and I haven't looked back.'

I nodded approvingly. 'Your mother sounds like a smart woman.'

'She is,' Natasha agreed.

'And you met Ethan doing an orienteering course?'

'Yes – Grace and I went along at the last minute,' she said. I could hear the happiness in her voice at the memory. 'That's got to be fate, right?'

'Sounds like it.'

'Ethan and I started seeing each other the weekend after that – he invited me up to London to have lunch, and we couldn't stop talking. It was like we'd always known each other.'

'What does he do?'

'Consulting with various start-ups, things like that. It's his own business, which is great because he understands the issues I'm often faced with,' she said. 'Sometimes it's difficult if we've both got a lot of work on at the same time, but we've got big plans for our future, so it's worth it.'

Listening to her, I couldn't help but feel resolved to do all I could to keep her safe for the next twenty-four hours. She was charming, effervescent and full of life and as she regaled me with stories about some of the places she and Ethan had travelled to since their first fateful meeting a year ago, and all of the adventures they'd had together, I suddenly wanted them to have many more years ahead of them to live their lives to the fullest.

We looked up at a shout from Ava to see her directing the stretcher bearers to lower Noah, and then she beckoned to me.

'Your turn,' she said. 'It's the last half mile, and then we'll be able to set up the tents and start dinner.'

'Thank goodness for that,' said Sarah, digging her knuckles into her back. 'I'm starving.'

As I took my side of the stretcher alongside Ava and started to move forward, my stomach flipped, but it wasn't from hunger.

I was wondering how on earth I was going to keep Natasha safe overnight so she could be reunited with her family the next day.

CHAPTER THIRTY-ONE

The rain had eased to a typical English drizzle by the time we reached the camp site.

The stream gurgled with fresh run-off from the surrounding hills, and its waters lapped at the exposed granite rock that protruded out from under lush green grass hassocks. Here and there, fallen branches cluttered the banks, gathering rotten leaves and other debris that had been washed downstream in the storm.

Ava directed everyone where to set up their tents, with all of them clustered under a canopy of Scots pine trees several metres from the stream. We were high enough on a natural rise in case it broke its banks overnight and close enough to fetch water for cooking.

I made a point of pitching mine so that it faced

Natasha's – I wanted to be able to see anyone entering or leaving her tent, and I planned to stay awake as long as possible, fuelled by the strong coffee that Noah and I were making. I had two energy drinks in the side pockets of my backpack as well, and what with four muesli bars and a large slab of chocolate, I reckoned I would be all right until the first tentative rays of light poked their way into our camp at around eight o'clock the next morning.

I hoped.

The tents ready, we set about creating a three-sided shelter beside the fire, so we had somewhere dry to sit and eat. After Ava checked the structure, making adjustments where needed and adding more pine branches to ward off the rain, she joined us and reassured the hen party that once Noah was safely back at the activities centre, it would be business as usual.

'You're not scheduled to leave us until five tomorrow afternoon,' she said. 'If we start early tomorrow as planned, then we might have time to do some axe throwing after the archery before you go.'

Sarah waggled her eyebrows theatrically at Natasha. 'Reckon you can trust me with sharp objects?'

The bride-to-be laughed. 'I hope so – one accident this weekend is enough, thank you.'

Goosebumps flecked my arms at their words, and I shuffled closer to Noah, lowering my voice. 'Are you sure that's a good idea?'

'We have to give them their money's worth,' he said. 'As it is, Ava overheard Grace telling Emily that she's thinking about giving us a bad review online after this afternoon's events.'

'But...'

'It's already been decided,' said Noah. 'Executive decision.'

'I'm here to look after my client's daughter,' I hissed. 'It doesn't help if you lot keep putting potential obstacles in my way – especially if those obstacles are dangerous.'

'They'll be supervised at all times.' He broke another branch in half and fed it into the fire. 'It'll be fine.'

I glared at him but abandoned the conversation as the women moved closer to the fire, holding out tin mugs for coffee, and murmuring their approval as the hot liquid eased the chills from their bones. Sipping mine, I warmed my hands around the mug and moved along the shelter to where Emily sat a little away from the others, her eyes unfocused as she stared at the flames.

'You must be excited about next weekend,' I said. 'It's not every day your brother gets married, after all.'

She blinked, as if noticing me for the first time, then forced a smile. 'Yes, I suppose so.'

'You don't seem sure. Everything okay?'

'I guess.' She gave a shrug. 'It'll be weird not having him around. He and Natasha are buying a flat.'

I frowned. 'I didn't know he still lived at home.'

'He doesn't,' she said. 'He and a friend rent a place in Islington, but he spends most of his weekends with us – it's quieter at home, and he's got more interests in the countryside than in the city.'

'Where are they buying their flat?'

'Manchester. He says it'll be better for his business, and for Natasha's. It puts them in a central location in case they need to meet in person with their clients and distributors, and of course it's got an airport so they can go anywhere they like. Besides, they'll have places like this on their doorstep to explore.'

She sounded glum, and in the reflection from the fire, I saw her brow furrow.

'You're going to miss him, aren't you?' I ventured.

'Yes.' She wiped at her eyes, then sniffed. 'But that's selfish of me, isn't it? He's head over heels about Natasha, and it's good to see him happy again. I thought after…'

'What are you two talking about?'

I looked up as Isabella joined us, crouching beside Emily and stroking her hair.

'Are you okay?'

'I'm fine, Mum. Stop worrying.' Emily got up and moved away, wandering over to join Natasha who had produced a pack of playing cards from her backpack and seemed to be walloping everybody at poker.

Isabella shook her head as she watched her go. 'It's so hard watching them grow up.'

'I take it she and Ethan are close,' I said.

'They always have been,' she said wistfully. 'And she's finding it hard to adjust to the idea that he's moving away.'

'They'll keep in touch though, won't they? And she and Natasha seem to get on well.'

'True, but you know what it's like – Ethan and Natasha have their own lives to lead. He and Emily will grow apart eventually.'

'What about you? Are you looking forward to the wedding?'

Her smile seemed forced when she replied. 'Of course I am. I just hope...'

I let the silence spin out for a moment, then frowned. 'Hope what?'

Isabella tossed the dregs of her coffee into the fire and sighed. 'I just hope that this time, there *is* a wedding.'

CHAPTER THIRTY-TWO

The fire was crackling and sending sparks up into the night sky by the time we prepared the food and started cooking. Ava, Noah and I had packed plastic boxes with meat and vegetarian options for the hen party, and soon the smell of sausages filled the air.

The rain had given way to a clear sky filled with stars, and in between turning the food to make sure it didn't get cremated, I watched while Natasha, Grace and Emily sat on a tumble of granite boulders a little way off from the firelight and pointed out different constellations.

Sarah sat on the opposite side of the fire to me, scrolling through photographs and videos she had taken that day, and Isabella was standing next to the tents with Ava, their heads bowed while they spoke in low voices.

I looked up as Noah hobbled over. 'How are you feeling?'

'Better after some rest and painkillers,' he quipped. He sat beside me and stared into the flames. 'Actually, a lot better than I did earlier. It's getting easier to put my weight on my foot, so I reckon by the morning I'll be over the worst.'

'That's good.' I meant it – I wanted us off the hills and back in the safety of the activities centre as soon as possible, and the longer we took to get there, the more nervous I would be. 'Right, I think these are done if you want to give everyone a shout.'

There was a polite stampede for the food, given that the hen party and guides had worked up voracious appetites with the extra and unforeseen exercise that had been undertaken using all of our reserves that afternoon. Natasha and her friends were complimentary about my cooking, so at least I felt I'd contributed something to the weekend other than a stretcher case in Noah, and we fell silent as we devoured the last of the foil-baked potatoes.

Ava licked her fingers, then put down her plate and eyed the group. 'How is everyone feeling after today?'

'Flatter,' Noah deadpanned, and winked at me.

'Sorry,' I said, to muted giggles from the others. It was good of him to make light of the situation, but I was keen to find out what Ava had in mind.

'Okay, so Noah's ankle isn't as bad as we thought after some rest,' she continued, looking around at each of the hen party in turn. 'How do you feel about an earlier start than planned so that we can aim to have you back at the activities centre by twelve tomorrow? That will then give you four to five hours of activities around the centre in the afternoon before the sun sets.'

'Sounds good to me,' said Natasha, nibbling on a piece of bacon. 'It'll be easier to drive south once the worst of the traffic has gone anyway.'

'I'm in,' said Grace. 'It makes a lot of sense.'

After Sarah, Emily and Isabella had added their agreement, Ava turned to Noah. 'I think we need to get everybody up by seven-thirty latest. The three of us can pack everything tonight to save time, so it'll just be the tents and sleeping bags in the morning.'

I stood up and started collecting empty plates. 'In that case, I'll wash up while you're doing that.'

'I'll give you a hand… oh, excuse me,' said Natasha, emitting an enormous yawn. 'Too much fresh air.'

'No such thing,' Isabella said good-naturedly. 'But I think we should all turn in – it's going to be a long day tomorrow.'

'I agree,' said Noah, struggling to his feet before waving away my offer of help. 'Does anyone need anything before we call it a night?'

I turned away while he hobbled over to each participant and helped them with various minor niggles with their camping equipment and switched on my head torch to make my way over to the stream.

As I rinsed the plates, marvelling at the rhythmic sound of the water bubbling over the rocks, I took a deep breath and exhaled. I knew then that I'd return to the Lake District one day, in better circumstances. Today had been challenging, and the weekend wasn't over yet, but I had fallen in love with the rugged landscape and beautiful views.

I whistled under my breath as I wandered back to the fire. Sarah and Grace were heading to their respective tents, and I smiled as Isabella gave Emily a hug before saying good night to everyone. Ava was checking the shelter again, ready for the morning, and Noah called out to Natasha, standing by the fire and warming her hands.

'Time to douse that,' he said. 'Do you want to do the honours?'

'Okay.' She crossed over to a bottle of water that had been left beside her backpack, and uncapped it, passing me as she returned.

I froze, then spun around, the words tumbling from my mouth as I ran towards her.

'No, don't!'

It was too late.

She tipped the contents over the fire, and then her eyes widened in horror as an almighty *whump* thundered the air and enormous flames shot upwards.

I launched myself at her, tackling her to the ground while sparks and splinters of wood showered us.

I could hear voices, screams, shouting, and then Ava and Noah were dragging us away, patting down our clothing as hot embers pierced the material.

Shaking, I rose to my feet and watched as the flames died down, then looked at Natasha.

She was pale, her porcelain features ghost-like in the firelight while Grace, Sarah, Emily and Isabella rushed over to comfort her.

'What happened?' Ava demanded.

Natasha shook her head, her voice trembling. 'All I was going to do was douse the flames, just like Noah said. So, I found some water.'

'It wasn't water,' I said, walking over to collect

the discarded plastic bottle before holding it aloft. 'Can't you smell it? It's petrol.'

CHAPTER THIRTY-THREE

Nobody knew where the bottle came from.

Natasha told us she had simply assumed it was one of ours from the time around the fire having dinner, but the label wasn't one from the water bottles in the activities centre's vending machine, and everyone else was carrying litre-sized sports bottles.

Or so they said.

I wasn't the police, so I couldn't demand that everybody empty their backpacks in front of me, and I wasn't yet ready to blow my cover, so I couldn't ask too many questions either.

Ava stalked around the perimeter of the camp site, peering over rocks and under shrubs in case there were any other bottles of petrol lying around, her features troubled while Noah soothed the hen party's nerves and coaxed them towards their tents, reminding them that there was still an early morning start to prepare for.

That done, he set about tidying away the camp, dousing the fire with a bottle of water he fetched from Ava's bag. He sniffed the contents before tipping them onto the flames and then packed away the cooking equipment while I applied some ointment from the first aid kit to a minor scorch mark on the back of my hand.

'Are you okay?' Ava said, dropping to a crouch beside me.

'Yes, thanks.' I waved the back of my hand at her. 'This looks worse than it feels.'

'Even so, keep it clean. That dressing will need changing in the morning before we head off.'

'Okay.'

She sighed. 'Look, I realise you and I started on the wrong foot when you turned up last week, but I just wanted to say well done. If you hadn't been there…'

'I know.' I shivered. 'And thanks.'

She lowered her head in response, then took the first aid kit from me. 'Best get to bed. I'll see you in the morning.'

'Sure. 'Night.'

"Night.'

I walked to my tent, my heart racing. I was sure more than ever that someone in the group was determined to stop Natasha getting to her wedding next weekend, and that person had come here prepared.

The petrol wasn't an accident. It was a premeditated act, and no matter what the others said about the bottle being left behind by other campers, I wasn't convinced.

Glancing over my shoulder, I saw each of Natasha's friends and future family hug her before she disappeared inside her tent and wondered who on earth would want to harm her, and why.

Smelling the petrol when she had walked past me with the bottle had been sheer luck. If the wind was blowing in the opposite direction, or if I hadn't been passing her right at that moment, the consequences would have been terrible.

Despite the remnant adrenaline still rushing around my system, I was yawning by the time I started to undress. In the light of my head torch, I shed my jacket and fleece, removed my waterproof walking trousers, and stuffed my socks into my boots to stop any bugs climbing inside.

That done, I climbed into my sleeping bag

wearing my base layers, shivering a little. I wasn't cold – the clothing and sleeping bag took care of that – I was scared, and I didn't mind admitting it.

Being here, in the middle of nowhere with a killer on the loose, was a lot different from carrying out online investigations about people's future spouses or even conducting surveillance from a safe distance.

'Pull yourself together, Harper,' I muttered.

I tugged the sleeping bag up around my shoulders and switched off my head torch before shuffling towards the tent opening, unzipping it a little so I could peer out without being seen. Sitting there staring at Natasha's tent, I felt around blindly until I found one of my energy drinks and popped the lid. The sugar smacked the back of my teeth and would enrage my dentist, but it did the trick. I soon stopped yawning and instantly felt more alert.

Which was just as well, because forty minutes later a shadowy figure slipped between the tents and crept towards the shelter where we'd stored the backpacks for the night.

I squinted in the low light from an overcast moon, trying to see their features, but then clouds scuttled across the sky, obscuring their face. They were wearing a dark woollen hat that covered their hair, and because of the angle I was unable to work out their height.

Then the thin sliver of moon re-emerged, and I gasped.

It was Ava, and she was leaning over the bags containing the abseiling ropes and harnesses.

'That's it, enough,' I muttered. I dived for my clothes, pulled them on, and wedged my feet back into my boots before tearing the tent flap open and hurrying over. 'What are you doing?'

Ava spun around to face me, her mouth open in surprise. 'You...'

'What are you doing?' I repeated.

'Double-checking the equipment, what does it look like?' she hissed. 'Why aren't you asleep?'

'Maybe because someone's sneaking around the camp and tampering with evidence,' I snapped. 'Your insurers are going to want to inspect all of that, aren't they?'

'That's why I'm making sure we've got everything.'

'You could have done that this evening – or first thing tomorrow before we leave.'

'What's going on?'

We both turned at the sound of Noah's voice.

'Ava was...' I began.

'Checking the ropes to make sure we've got them all, and the anchor that failed,' Ava finished. She held it up, its crooked angle sending a shiver down my spine. 'And before you ask, Melody, it's going in my backpack for safekeeping.'

'Well, keep your voices down,' said Noah. 'The pair of you will wake up everybody else at this rate.'

'I was heading back to my tent anyway,' Ava replied. 'I've still got the accident report to fill out before we sleep.'

'Melody, I suggest you go too.' Noah gave me a gentle shove. 'Sounds like Ava's got this all under control.'

Not wishing to draw attention to myself from Natasha and the others, I gave them a curt nod and turned on my heel.

I could feel Ava's gaze boring into my back as I stalked back to my tent.

CHAPTER THIRTY-FOUR

I woke up to a different robin blaring in my ear and a stiffness in my spine from the unfamiliar sleeping arrangements.

Sometime during the night, my exhaustion had taken hold, and I'd tumbled onto my side in my sleeping bag, my head resting on my daypack. Somewhere in there was a particularly lumpy object that had left an indent in my forehead, and while I groped around in the dark to find my head torch, I bit back a yawn. The last time I had looked at my phone screen was three o'clock, and evidently the energy drinks weren't living up to the description, because I didn't recall anything after that.

Panic seized me, and after dressing I unzipped the flap and peered out towards Natasha's tent.

She unzipped it and gave me a cheery wave before disappearing back inside, and I breathed a sigh of relief. The rest of the hen party was still asleep, so after dashing across to a secluded shrub to pee, I started packing up my things to get a head start on the day.

At seven o'clock, the hillside was peaceful, but as I walked over to the remnants of the campfire, I could still smell petrol.

Scuffing dirt over the ashes with my boots to make sure it didn't reignite after we left, I looked over my shoulder at the sound of approaching voices to see Ava and Noah. 'Morning.'

'Morning,' said Noah. He had some colour back in his face and was putting more weight on his injured ankle. 'Sleep okay?'

'Yes thanks.' All right, it was almost a lie, but right now, I didn't know who to trust.

Every single person in the camp site was a suspect, after all.

Ava was looking at the other tents. 'I'll give them another ten minutes, and then if they don't emerge, I'll go and wake them.'

'I'd put some coffee on, but in the circumstances we should probably get moving as soon as we're ready.' Noah gestured to the backpacks. 'Could you help me carry mine, Melody? I can walk, but the extra weight might be too much today.'

'Sure, no problem.'

Five minutes later, Isabella and Emily joined us looking no worse for wear. In fact, Isabella was radiant in the weak morning sunlight and evidently relished being out in the elements.

Natasha and Grace were next, chatting enthusiastically about the afternoon's planned activities.

After ten minutes, Ava checked her watch. 'I presume Sarah doesn't like early mornings.'

'Never has,' said Natasha, laughing. 'Do you want me to go and get her?'

'I will. You've still got to pack up your sleeping bag and everything.' Grace turned back to the remaining tents, calling over her shoulder. 'I'll give her a hand dismantling these too.'

I turned my attention back to the bags with the abseiling kit inside and wondered again what Ava had been up to last night. I was sure she was lying about why she was sneaking around the camp and going through the equipment, but I couldn't prove anything, and she hadn't tried to hide her intentions when Noah asked her.

Then a scream pierced the air, threatening to turn my insides to liquid.

Everybody froze, and then Grace burst from Sarah's tent, ran over to the trees fringing the camp site, and vomited.

She was crying by the time we scrambled from our position near the bags, her sobs wracking her body as Natasha reached her first, grasping her arms.

'What's wrong?' she urged. 'What's the matter?'

'It's… it's Sarah,' Grace blurted, tears streaking her face. 'Sh… she's dead.'

CHAPTER THIRTY-FIVE

Ava took charge, of course.

She ushered Grace over to the charred remains of the campfire, told everyone to stay there with Noah, then beckoned to me before stalking back to Sarah's tent.

'What do you want me to do? I gulped.

I'd never seen a dead body, and I wasn't looking forward to the prospect, especially as I'd only been chatting with Sarah the night before. It didn't seem possible that she was now dead.

'I'm going to check her vital signs,' Ava replied. She paused outside Sarah's tent and held my gaze. 'And I need a witness.'

'Right. Okay.' I tried to ignore the dread in my

stomach while she peered through the open flap and held my breath as she disappeared inside.

'Open the flap,' she called. 'I need you to watch me.'

I closed my eyes, for a moment, then straightened my shoulders and peered inside.

Ava was crouched next to Sarah's sleeping bag. The young woman's left arm lay stretched out from the confines of the thermal material and her hair was tumbled over her face. She looked like she was sleeping, except there was an eerie quiet in the tent.

Reaching out for Sarah's neck, Ava wrapped her fingers around the woman's wrist before rocking back onto her heels and sighing. 'She's gone.'

I swallowed. 'How?'

'I don't know. Did she say anything to you last night about feeling unwell?'

'No.'

Ava frowned. 'She didn't tell us about any food allergies or anything on her indemnity and waiver form yesterday. And I don't recall her notifying us of any health issues.'

I could still hear my heartbeat in my ears. 'What do we do?'

'Well, as far as the police will be concerned, this

is a crime scene, even if she has died from natural causes.'

'But how do we report it to them?' I said. 'We haven't got any mobile reception up here.'

'I'll have to use the radio to contact Chris and ask him to phone them.' Ava signalled to me to leave the tent and shuffled out after me, zipping shut the flap. She looked tired, and I wondered whether that was from the shock of seeing a dead body, or whether I should be worried that I was standing next to a cold-blooded killer who had spent the night prowling the camp site.

'Noah was only going to slow down our descent back to Tarrant's Cross today,' she added, 'so he can stay here until the police arrive.'

I peered past her to where the hen party and Noah were standing beside all the backpacks, watching us. 'What about Natasha and the rest of them? The police will want to interview them too, won't they?'

'You and I can guide them back to the activities centre,' she said. 'They'll be warmer there, and the police will find it easier to interview them there too, I think.'

I nodded. 'Makes sense. It'll save anyone tampering with evidence too, won't it?'

She raised an eyebrow. 'Evidence?'

'Evidence,' I reiterated. 'You said it yourself – Sarah didn't have any allergies or medical conditions, and she was absolutely fine when she went to bed last night. Natural causes or not, the police will want a forensic team up here as soon as possible.'

She looked worried then, and I narrowed my eyes at her.

'Is that going to be a problem?'

'No,' she said, then turned on her heel. 'I'm going to radio Chris now.'

I followed her back to the others and rested a hand on Grace's shoulder as I joined them, giving her a light squeeze, then turned to Natasha. 'I'm so sorry.'

She wiped away tears with the sleeve of her fleece, then gulped. 'I can't believe it. I just can't believe it. Are you sure?'

'We're sure,' said Ava.

'I want to see her,' said Natasha.

'I'm sorry, but I can't let you do that.' Ava explained about the police, and I watched as the women paled.

'Are you saying somebody murdered her?' said Isabella, a wobble to her voice while she looked at her daughter, and then the others.

'No, I'm saying the police will want us to leave her alone until they can get here. In the meantime,

Melody and I are going to get you back to the activities centre where it's warm and dry while we wait for them to turn up.'

'But we can't just leave her here,' Emily blurted.

'Noah can stay behind and look after her,' I said gently. 'She won't be on her own.'

Natasha fell to her knees, sobbing. 'This is all my fault. What was I thinking dragging you all out here?'

I thought about her near miss yesterday when I'd taken her place to climb up the crag, then about the accident with the petrol on the fire last night.

I couldn't think of any words to comfort her.

CHAPTER THIRTY-SIX

Sarah's mobile phone was missing.

Ava, Noah and I made a collective decision that one of us would enter Sarah's tent before decamping and remove any valuables to take back to Tarrant's Cross with us in case Noah had to leave before the police arrived. As a qualified mountain first aider, he would be obliged to help any passing hikers that needed help, despite our own terrible circumstances.

Except that when Ava slipped on a pair of nitrile gloves from the first aid kit and carefully went through Sarah's daypack next to her body, there was no mobile phone.

'Her purse is here though,' said Ava, holding up a fabric wallet with a surf company's logo emblazoned across the front.

'Is it underneath her?' I ventured. 'She might've rolled over in her sleep before...'

'I daren't move her,' Ava replied. 'I could get into real trouble for that, couldn't I?'

She was right, of course. Any detective who turned up later today would not treat us favourably if their crime scene was disturbed.

'Can you run your hand underneath her or something instead?' Noah said, then shrugged. 'That's not really moving her, is it?'

Ava pondered his suggestion for a moment and then knelt down again. 'Okay, here goes. At least I've got you two here as witnesses, right?'

Witnesses.

It suddenly hit me that I might have to remember all of this for a future court appearance and yet here I was, watching one of my potential suspects tampering with a murder victim.

'It's not here.' She stood up and waved us from the tent. 'We need to get our guests back before the weather turns again, and we need to report this before we go.'

Ava radioed Chris while Noah and I helped the women finish packing, ending her call with a curt response before handing the radio to Noah.

'Chris will let you know when the police have

reached the activities centre,' she said. 'It could be a while because the nearest local patrol is over in Ambleside, and then I'll have to guide them back here.'

'Okay.' He looked over his shoulder at the sole remaining tent before turning back to us. 'Be safe.'

Leaving the camp was a sombre affair, with Ava leading the way back up the winding path we had followed the previous day and me bringing up the rear.

I watched the five people in front of me with a sickening twist in my stomach. Four of them were potential suspects, and I was meant to be guarding the other so that she came to no harm.

It could have been Natasha who had died last night instead of Sarah after I had fallen asleep whilst on watch. If I had stayed awake, I might have seen who had crept into Sarah's tent and murdered her, but now I was faced with the terrifying prospect that her killer was right here with us – and the police were hours away.

The other women were quiet, their heads down while they trudged in a single file behind Ava. Isabella was in front of the others, her long strides keeping up with the guide while Emily followed in her wake. Natasha was next, and even over the stiff breeze that whipped around us I could hear her sniffing from time to time. Grace was in front of me, silent for the most part but hurrying to catch up with Natasha now and again, resting a soothing hand on her arm before dropping back when the path narrowed once more.

I spent the time wracking my brain for answers, subdued by the sudden loss of somebody I'd considered a suspect in sabotaging yesterday's climb and responsible for the incident with the campfire last night.

But why had Sarah been murdered?

Did she have her own suspicions about the mysterious coincidences, or did she accidentally stumble across the killer on the way to Natasha's tent?

I stopped in my tracks and looked over my shoulder to where Sarah's tent was now hidden amongst thick woodland below us, the stream a thin sparkling ribbon in the morning light.

What if Noah was the killer?

Had I just left behind Natasha's murderer, free to remove any evidence from the crime scene before the police got there? Had he taken Sarah's phone?

Why?

What was on there that was so important?

'Melody, hurry up,' Ava called.

I turned to see her waiting at the top of the rise, the others almost there, and raised a hand in response before hurrying to join them. She gave me a curious look, but I shook my head. I wasn't prepared to discuss anything with anybody right now.

Instead, I pulled my phone from my pocket while the rest of the group set off again and sighed. There was still no signal.

'Ava says it'll be another six miles before we can use them,' said Grace after I caught up with her. 'And even then, it can be pretty dodgy.'

'I'm sure we'll know when there's a signal. Our phones will be pinging like crazy when all those notifications pop up at once.'

She gave a wan smile before increasing her pace, leaving me alone and worried.

There had been two attempts on Natasha's life already, and if Sarah hadn't been murdered we would have been out in these hills for several hours today. Now we were heading back and still two, maybe three hours away from Tarrant's Cross at the pace Ava was setting.

Did that mean the killer would panic and escalate their attempts to harm her?

I fell behind, lost in thought while wondering how I was going to ensure that Natasha survived the rest of the day.

CHAPTER THIRTY-SEVEN

Ava had been right.

Six miles later, my phone emitted a series of trills and pings, echoed by everyone else's and sounding very much out of place in the rugged landscape.

'Let's have a five-minute break,' Ava said. 'And may I suggest you tell nobody about what's happened until the police tell us we can.'

'That should include Sarah's parents,' said Natasha, looking at Grace and then her future family. 'It's going to be hard enough for them to find out, without us blurting it out like this. I want to be with them when I speak to them.'

The others acquiesced, and I removed myself over to a pile of granite boulders that provided a panoramic view of the valley. I could see the roof of the activities centre in the far distance, nestled amongst oak, beech and horse chestnut trees that were losing the last of their golden brown leaves, and Lake Windermere beyond that.

It felt like a lifetime since I'd arrived at the train station, but it was only three days. Three days that had inexorably changed my life, and that of those around me, forever.

I sat on the uppermost rock and peered at my phone screen, scrolling through the notifications and dismissing anything that could wait. I was left with two emails – one from Patricia Berriminster that turned out to be a signed copy of the contract I had emailed to her on Tuesday with apologies for the delay, and the other was from Shaun Hendrick.

There was no text, just a capitalised subject line that read: CALL ME ASAP.

And he had left a voicemail message.

'Harper, it's Shaun. Phone me the minute you get this. It's urgent.'

The automated service informed me that he had left the message last night at seven o'clock, and from the background noise, it sounded like he had been at work.

I hit the callback button.

He answered before the second ring. 'You were meant to check in last night and this morning.'

'There's no signal out here. We've only just got one now that we're heading back to Tarrant's Cross.'

'How's it going?' he said. 'Everything all right?'

'Ask me another question.'

'What's wrong?'

I looked across to where Ava and Isabella were talking, the older woman hugging her arms to her chest while she listened. 'I'll have to tell you when we get back to the activities centre. It's complicated.'

'Is Natasha okay?'

'Yes.' Checking over my shoulder to make sure nobody was nearby who could overhear me, I turned away from the wind to better hear his voice. 'What's so urgent?'

'I did some digging around yesterday afternoon while I was waiting for a suspect to be brought in for questioning on one of my cases,' he explained. 'I wanted to know more about Helen Dumois's death.'

My heart skipped a beat. 'And? What did you find out?'

'Nothing. The file's been locked down.'

'Locked down? What does that mean?'

'It means I can't access it on our system to read

what went on with the original investigation. Someone's revoked my access.' I heard his chair creak as he leaned forward, picturing him running his hand though his hair as he talked. 'In fact, none of us have access to it. I had one of my colleagues take a look, and she can't open it either.'

I frowned. 'That doesn't make sense.'

'I know, and I don't want to raise a ticket with our IT lot until I find out why.'

'Okay, can you let me know if you manage to find out anything?'

'I will, but there's more.'

I caught movement out of the corner of my eye and saw Grace beckoning to me to hurry up. The other three were already on their way, making steady progress along the track that wound a zigzagging path down the hillside. 'You're going to have to be quick, Hendrick – we've got another hour or more before we get back to Tarrant's Cross, and we're setting off now.'

'I can't find any record of Ava Thomas prior to the time of her arrival as a staff member at the activities centre.'

I nearly dropped the phone. 'Pardon?'

'She doesn't exist. Her name doesn't appear anywhere on any of our partners' databases, she doesn't have anything on her social media profiles older than three years ago, and every single one of her posts is about her time there at Tarrant's Cross. Nothing personal, and nobody in the background of her photos either. She hasn't even followed anybody back so I can't delve into her friends' backgrounds either.'

I watched while Ava threaded her way between gorse and bare hawthorn bushes, her gait determined. 'Maybe she was married and got divorced or something.'

'Nope, I checked all of those records as well. She's a ghost, Harper.'

'That can't be right.'

'It gets worse.'

'Brilliant,' I said, unable to keep the sarcasm from my voice. 'What?'

'Noah Weller has a juvenile record that's sealed.'

'Sealed? So you can't see what he was charged for?'

'I can't, but I called in a favour with a colleague in Cumbria Police.' Hendrick lowered his voice. 'And this is strictly off the record, understand?'

'Loud and clear.'

'She said that Noah had a violent streak as a

teenager and landed another lad in a coma for three weeks after punching them outside their school.'

'Great. Just what I needed to hear.' I rubbed my temple, then exhaled. 'Look, I couldn't tell you just now because I was surrounded, but one of the hen party was murdered last night. Sarah Llewellyn. One of the others found her dead in her tent this morning, and her phone was taken. Ava is leading us back down to Tarrant's Cross so she can meet the police there before guiding them up to where we camped.'

'What?'

'Yes, and that was after two accidents that I'm sure were intended to kill Natasha. I can't prove anything though, Hendrick,' I said, frustrated. 'I've got no evidence, just hunches.'

'Then you need to be careful. Even when you get back to Tarrant's Cross.'

'But the police are coming. Surely the murderer won't be desperate enough to try something while they're crawling all over the place, will they?'

'Whoever the killer is, they murdered Sarah and stole her phone to stop her saying anything,' Hendrick pointed out. 'So, what do you think?'

I closed my eyes. 'I think you might be right.'

'I do, too. Hold on.' There was movement in the background, then voices and he lowered the phone for a moment before returning. 'I've got to go, there's a briefing in five minutes I need to attend. Be careful, Harper. Somebody doesn't want Natasha Berriminster to make it to her wedding, and you're the only one standing in their way.'

CHAPTER THIRTY-EIGHT

I hadn't been wrong in my assumption that the activities centre at Tarrant's Cross would have a heavy police presence when we got back.

As we wound our way through the woodland path and the trees thinned closer to the main track leading to the house, I could see three liveried patrol cars parked in the yard alongside a plain white panel van and a green hatchback car that had seen better days.

There was a uniformed constable standing on the threshold watching our progress, his face grim before he ducked his chin to the radio on his stab vest and announced our imminent arrival.

By the time I reached the yard, a man in a grey suit and pale blue shirt had joined him, together with a taller uniformed man with sergeant's stripes on his epaulettes. The man in the suit wore an impatient expression while his tie flapped in the wind, his hands on his hips.

'Which one of you is Ava Thomas?' he asked as we slipped our backpacks to the ground and eased our aching shoulders.

'I am,' she said, her voice wary. 'And you are?'

'Detective Sergeant Samuel Drayton, Cumbria Police. I've already interviewed your colleague Chris Weller so while we're interviewing the rest of you, he can show my team where to find this camp site of yours. I want a word with you now, please.'

He waved her inside, and I watched as she followed the uniformed sergeant. Then Drayton turned to the rest of us. 'We're going to split you up and take your statements, ladies. Apologies, I realise you're mourning the loss of your friend, but once these interviews are done I can leave you in peace.'

'Could we freshen up first?' asked Grace. 'I need the loo.'

'One at a time,' Drayton replied. 'And make it quick.'

Natasha sniffed, and Grace placed an arm around her shoulder, but both stayed silent.

'Where do you want us?' I asked, picking up my backpack.

'Wait in the guest lounge,' came the reply. 'You'll find a constable there who will answer any questions you've got about the interview process, and we'll do those in the kitchen. Do any of you want a solicitor to be present?'

Emily reached out for Isabella's hand, her mouth open.

Reality had set in for the four friends, and I was keen for Drayton to hear my side of the story before he spoke to the others.

'No,' Natasha said. 'We don't.'

I held up my hand. 'I'll go first.'

Chris passed me in the reception area wearing a warm fleece, lightweight jacket and trousers. His eyes were full of concern, but he said nothing as he stalked towards the front door, merely giving me a slight nod before his attention was taken by three men dressed in casual clothes who emerged from the kitchen.

Two of them carried bulky canvas bags with them and when one knelt to unzip a compartment on the side, I spotted protective coveralls encased in plastic ready to be used. I swallowed uneasily.

The white panel van evidently belonged to DS

Drayton's forensic specialists, and when I heard the third man talking on his phone as he walked outside, I realised he was the pathologist brought in to formally confirm Sarah's death.

The remaining members of the hen party filed in through the front door next wearing stunned expressions as they headed for the living room. I heard muted voices, including a rich baritone that must have belonged to the constable stationed there, and then Grace emerged, pale, wiping at fresh tears.

DS Drayton hurried inside before she could say anything to me though, and she sniffed before turning towards the toilets.

'I take it you're Melody Harper?' Drayton began.

'Yes.'

'Okay, come with me – like I said, we'll use the kitchen to do the interviews given it's far enough away from the living room to avoid being overheard.'

I frowned as I followed him, then realised Chris must've told him who I was, and what I was doing there.

The detective held open the kitchen door for me, closing it behind us, and it was then that I spotted the uniformed sergeant already sitting at the dining table, his expression one of curiosity. There was a recording gadget next to him, and an A4-sized notebook and pen primed and ready.

'You can put your backpack on the floor over there,' said Drayton before gesturing to a chair on the opposite side of the table. 'Take a seat. Would you like some water?'

My gaze fell on the kettle on the hob, then on the two ceramic mugs on the table, telltale brown tide marks inside both. 'Could I have a coffee, please? I don't mind making it, but it's cold out there and I really need to warm up.'

'Go on then.' Drayton gathered the mugs together and plonked them on the worktop beside the coffee jar. 'Mine's black with one, and Harris here likes a splash of milk in his.'

Cheeky.

Still, it seemed I wasn't in any trouble given Drayton's tone, and my shoulders had relaxed a little by the time I passed over the coffees and took my place at the table. Wrapping my hands around the mug after taking a tentative sip and deciding it was too hot to drink straight away, I leaned back in my seat.

'Thanks, I'm ready now.'

'Good. We'll do this officially, for the record,' said Drayton, then proceeded to recite the formal caution before continuing. 'Can you confirm your name and occupation please?'

'Melody Harper, private investigator.'

'And why are you here in Tarrant's Cross, Melody?'

'I was approached by my client, Patricia Berriminster, on Tuesday to pose as a guide working at this activities centre and to keep a close watch on her daughter, Natasha, who's here on a hen weekend. Mrs Berriminster told me that the groom's last fiancée disappeared without a trace, and she was worried about Natasha's safety. I found out yesterday morning that Helen Dumois, the previous fiancée, had died here at Tarrant's Cross four years ago during an outdoor activities event. Her death was ruled as accidental by the coroner at the time.'

Drayton nodded as he listened, while the sergeant did a good job of keeping up with me while he took notes. 'Had you met any of the hen party before today?'

'No.' I took a sip of coffee. 'I wasn't provided with their names by my client and only found out that Isabella Kingsley would be joining them the day before I arrived here, on Tuesday.'

'Why did you come here on Wednesday, when the rest of the hen party wasn't due to arrive on Friday?'

'I've never done anything like this before and they needed time to train me. Patricia, Mrs Berriminster, did some charity work or something with this place last year and said they owed her a favour. Patricia came up with the idea that I pose as a guide in order to keep an eye on her daughter and ensure she came to no harm. I arrived on Wednesday so I could spend some time learning about the tuition principles behind the activities the real guides here had planned for the weekend.'

Drayton mimicked my pose and leaned back in his chair, eyeing me with interest. 'Tell me what happened after they arrived.'

I took another sip of coffee, then a deep breath.

I kept to the facts and missed out nothing. I told Drayton about the failed anchor point in the rock face, and the bottle of petrol that somebody had left beside Natasha's backpack. And I told him about Sarah's phone being missing.

Half an hour later, only the sound of the sergeant's pen scratching his notebook filled the room and the rest of my coffee had gone cold.

Drayton waited for a moment, then leaned forward and clasped his hands on the table. 'What are your impressions about this place?'

'It's rustic, but clean.'

'Well run?'

I sighed. 'I think they mean well, but... one accidental death, and a murder? Both linked to Ethan Kingsley? I'm starting to wonder about the people running the place. I've tried to find out more about Ava Thomas, but there's nothing on any of the online resources available to me – she just doesn't exist beyond three years ago. Then there's Noah Weller, who's apparently got a violent past. Chris is difficult to read.'

'And the hen party?'

'Well, the only link between the two deaths is the Kingsleys.' I shrugged. 'I don't know – maybe they don't want Ethan to get married.'

Drayton leaned back and scratched his chin for a moment, then reached out to the recording equipment. 'Interview terminated at one forty-three PM. Miss Harper, you can leave but I will warn you not to discuss this interview with the others, is that understood?'

'Understood, yes.'

'Thank you for your time. I may need to speak to you again this afternoon, so please don't leave the property.'

CHAPTER THIRTY-NINE

Four faces turned to look at me when I walked into the guest lounge.

One of those was a burly constable who pointed to the far end of the room where the bar area was, keen to keep me separated from those who hadn't yet provided a statement.

Natasha, Emily and Grace were sitting on the sofas around the hearth, a roaring fire in the grate belching a warmth into the room that didn't quell the chill that crossed my shoulders.

Natasha looked shattered, her face pale as she turned away and watched the flames. She had come perilously close to meeting the same fate as Helen Dumois but had no idea how or why she was in danger.

Once DS Drayton told her, I feared she would be even more distraught at losing Sarah.

Grace sat beside her with her hands clasped over her knees, a stunned expression etched into her features. She stared at the carpet, unable to look at the young woman sitting opposite her.

Emily Kingsley was nervous, nibbling at a thumbnail and looking first at Grace, then Natasha as if willing them to meet her gaze.

Both ignored her.

There was a rumble from the bar, and I glanced over to see that Chris or Ava had set up a coffee urn with a jumbled collection of mugs beside it. Steam emanated from the lid while it reheated the contents, and the aroma was too enticing to resist. Wandering over, I poured a fresh brew, found a carton of milk in the small refrigerator under the bar, and sat on one of the stools facing away from the fire and shivered as the damp in my clothes started to dry out. I pulled out my phone, checking for any new messages from Shaun Hendrick.

There were none, and I bit back my disappointment.

I wanted to know more about Ava, and the more I thought about it, the more I wondered what her connection was to the Kingsleys. After all, I'd spotted her and Isabella in conversation by themselves more than once this weekend, speaking in low voices away from the rest of us. Prior to the hen party turning up, Ava had mysteriously disappeared off to Hawkshead on Friday, much to Chris and Noah's surprise. And who had been the one to set the anchors into the cliff face yesterday morning?

Ava.

She wasn't here, and I wondered whether she had merely gone back to her room after her interview, or whether the police were still speaking with her.

I sighed, then took a tentative sip of coffee.

It was perfect, and I closed my eyes while I savoured the rich flavour before it went cold like the last one had.

A melodic ringtone interrupted my contemplation, and I glanced over my shoulder to see Natasha lean forward and snatch up her phone from the coffee table.

'Wait.' The policeman was holding out his hand. 'I'm sorry, Miss Berriminster, but I'm under strict instructions not to let any of you take calls.'

'It's my mum,' said Natasha. 'She'll be worried. I was meant to call her as soon as we got back to Tarrant's Cross to let her know I'm okay.'

The constable sighed. 'Put it on speaker.'

'Mum?' She said, then burst into tears once more. Grace reached out and squeezed her hand before Natasha uncurled herself from the sofa. Hugging her fleece around her, she wandered over to a corner of the room where a shelf laden with second-hand books lined the wall, the constable in her wake before returning to her call. 'It's awful, Mum…'

I tuned out, seeking solace in my coffee dregs. I figured I'd finish my drink, then ask the constable standing by the door if I could be excused to get a hot shower and a change of clothes. At least I could pack my things and be ready to return to Windermere station once DS Drayton released us.

My phone buzzed then, vibrating across the wooden surface of the bar, and I saw the name "Mama Bear" on the screen. I looked over my shoulder to see Natasha back on the sofa beside Grace, then snatched up my phone and hurried over to the policeman. 'Can I take this outside? It's a private call.'

He nodded, and stood to one side to let me pass, given that I had already provided a statement, and I answered the call before it went to voicemail.

'Mrs Berriminster?'

'You see, I was right.'

I could hear the accusatory tone in her voice and

decided to be as diplomatic as possible. 'You were, Mrs Berriminster. Thank goodness you had the foresight to ask me to come this weekend.'

'What happened?'

'I'll be able to give you a full briefing tomorrow,' I said, pushing through the front door and stepping out into the windswept yard. I wished I'd had the sense to bring my jacket but there hadn't been time. 'We're still being interviewed by the police at the moment.'

'Yes, Natasha said she couldn't say much because the police were listening to our call. What's all that about?'

'She hasn't yet provided a formal statement, and the constable looking after them allowed her to speak to you as a courtesy,' I said, pacing the concrete hardstanding whilst side-stepping fresh rabbit droppings. 'He's not allowed to let them take calls until after they've been interviewed by the detective who's here.'

'I see.'

'Did you know that Helen Dumois died here at Tarrant's Cross?' I asked.

'I…' There was a coughing fit at the other end of the line before she recovered. 'I'd heard a rumour.'

'A rumour?'

'Well, we... That is, Peter and I did our own research about Ethan Kingsley and found out that he'd been engaged before. We wanted to know why.' She paused. 'I mean, that's what you do as a wedding detective, isn't it? Look into people's backgrounds. We just did the same.'

'You could've told me,' I said, gripping my phone harder and trying not to grind my teeth. 'I could've been better prepared.'

'You wouldn't have taken the job,' she said. 'Would you?'

I stopped pacing and turned to stare at the house. I knew what my answer would have been on Tuesday, but now?

'See?' Patricia continued. 'That's why I couldn't tell you about our fears. I thought that if I simply told you Ethan's last fiancée disappeared, you wouldn't be able to resist the mystery. I figured I'd just let you work it out for yourself.'

'I would've been in a better position to protect your daughter if you'd told me the whole story.'

'But what if I was wrong?' she said. 'As I said, we'd only heard a rumour, and we couldn't corroborate it, not without the access to systems that somebody like you has. So, it made more sense to us to ensure Natasha had a bodyguard with her who could protect her. And you did. For that, we'll be forever in your debt, Melody. I mean that.'

Hearing the sincerity and relief in her voice, my frustration dissolved in an instant. 'Look, I'm glad I could help. I just wish I could've protected Sarah too. I'll never forgive myself for that.'

'You're not a superhero, Melody. You did the best you could in extreme circumstances,' she scolded. 'And Natasha has told me everything about how you saved her life this weekend.'

'Thank you.' I checked the time at the top of the screen, then exhaled. 'I'd better go, just in case DS Drayton wants to speak to me again. The interviews are taking a while but I'm sure once he's spoken to Natasha she'll be released so she can make her way home.'

'Well, her father's on the way to pick her up. The taxi left two hours ago, so with any luck he'll be there in a few hours so he can drive her home. I can't imagine she's in any fit state to drive herself.'

I did a mental calculation at how much a taxi firm in my local area would charge me to drive to the Lake District, then realised for some people like the Berriminsters, money wasn't quite the same issue as it was for me, and figured I would do the same in the current circumstances.

'I'll look out for him in case he arrives while she's being interviewed,' I said.

'I'd appreciate that. Now, I'll let you get on. I'll speak with you tomorrow.'

'You will.'

Ending the call, I looked up at the hills where we had been hiking only a few hours before. Where once I'd seen a rugged beauty now seemed ominous in the fading afternoon light. When we had set off yesterday morning, I'd thought Patricia Berriminster and I would be proven wrong about there being a threat to Natasha's life.

How wrong I had been.

Cloud shadows loomed over the folds of granite rock and scrub-covered heath, and I realised that even with the aid of the four-wheel-drive vehicles, Chris, Noah and the police wouldn't be back for at least another three or four hours, not with the forensic team having to conduct their investigation while they waited.

My gaze fell on the large barn where all the equipment was kept on the far side of the yard, and then to the front door of the lodge. The policeman who had been standing at the front door awaiting our arrival was now overseeing the hen party in the guest lounge, and there was nobody else around.

I narrowed my eyes as I peered at the barn once more, then thought of the extra equipment I had left in my room before yesterday's hike.

There was no need for me to return to the guest lounge now that I had provided my statement to DS Drayton, and he would be busy for at least another hour or so.

I could be in and out within fifteen minutes. I only needed a couple of minutes to pick the padlock on the barn door, and Noah had told me the combination for the internal locked room because it was the same code he used for the ammunition safe.

I wasn't interested in that.

I wanted the personnel files.

I wanted to know why Shaun Hendrick was convinced Ava Thomas hadn't existed prior to coming to Tarrant's Cross.

CHAPTER FORTY

My set of stainless-steel lock picks had been a present from Charlie when I'd moved into the office above the fish and chip shop.

He had presented them to me with a shy smile after helping me carry the component parts of a flat-packed desk up the narrow staircase, and we had set about testing them on all the locks in the building while I honed my skills. When I had asked him how he had learned how to pick locks, he confessed to a misspent youth and an uncle who was currently serving a four-year stretch for breaking and entering.

I hadn't asked any further questions after that.

Now, I hurried back to my room, palmed the nylon wallet containing the picks into the pocket of my fleece and waited until the policeman leaning against the desk in the reception area had wandered back to the guest lounge before I lunged for the front door.

Ducking under the window as I passed the lounge, I ran to the barn and dropped to a crouch. The padlock was new, but a brand I had practised on. My hands shook as I selected a pick and a tension tool from the wallet. I had never done this for real before – it was illegal, after all, unless I was using them on my own property or with somebody's permission – but I was desperate.

I needed answers, because I felt sure the killer would make another attempt on Natasha's life before the wedding, and I wasn't convinced that Detective Sergeant Samuel Drayton was going to find out who that was in time.

At least that's what I told myself as I felt the final pin lift, the cylinder turn, and the shackle give way, releasing the lock.

Then I heard voices approaching, male, and looked behind me to see two of the constables rounding the far end of the drystone wall to the yard, their attention taken by the view behind them of Lake Windermere glistening in the distance.

I slapped the hasp of the padlock around, so it looked as if it was still in place, then hared across the yard to where Noah and Ava's four-wheel drives were parked and slewed to a crouch behind them, my insides twisting.

I hadn't realised two of the policemen weren't inside the house but when I risked a quick glance around the bumper of Noah's vehicle, I saw a wisp of smoke escape above their heads and realised that rather than patrolling the activities centre, the two officers had merely stepped outside for a cigarette break.

I held my breath while they drew closer to the barn. I hadn't wanted to pick the lock again because I was aware that at some point, I'd be reported missing from the house and was running out of time to get into the safe room, but I was now ruing my decision.

What if the policemen decided to check it?

One of them turned his head my way and I ducked, closing my eyes as if that would ward off any chance of being discovered.

Then I heard a laugh and raised my head to see the pair of them passing by the vehicles, too busy talking about yesterday's football score to take any notice of the barn. I breathed a sigh of relief as, finally, they scuffed their cigarette butts into the dirt and disappeared back inside the house.

I raced back to the barn, opened the door enough

to squeeze in, then put the padlock back on its hasp and pulled the door shut.

It was gloomy inside, and I felt a chill over my shoulders at the memory of the sound I'd heard on Friday when I had been in here with Noah learning about the clay pigeon shooting, not entirely convinced it was a cat instead of a giant rat. I daren't switch on the lights and give myself away though, so I felt in my pocket for my phone and swiped on the torch app. It provided enough light to see where I wanted to go without tripping over anything, but I would have to be careful.

The pigeons cooed from their vantage point in the rafters, but there were no other sounds, and I took a tentative step forward.

Then there was an almighty *creak* that plunged my heart to my stomach a split second later.

I spun around as the door squeaked on its hinges, then gave a sigh of relief when I realised the wind was pulling and pushing against it. It was too heavy to blow right open and give somebody out there cause for concern though, and I told myself to get on with my search before I was reported missing.

Walking over to the safe room, I eyed the digital lock and paused, replaying my conversation with Chris when we returned the shotguns on Friday afternoon. I quickly crossed my fingers, then tapped in the code he had given me for the gun cabinet.

Two, one, seven, four, seven, six.

Nothing happened.

I frowned, then spotted the hashtag in the bottom righthand corner of the keypad and pressed it.

There was a buzzing sound, and then the lock released with a resounding *click*.

Once inside, I pushed the door until it was almost closed, but not quite, just in case I needed to make a quick exit, and flipped on the light switch, hedging my bets that it wouldn't be seen from outside the barn.

Ignoring the metal wardrobe-like cabinet, I made my way over to the filing cabinet where Noah had told me all the centre's paperwork was kept and pulled out the top drawer.

I groaned under my breath.

None of the dark green hanging files inside were labelled, and so I began thumbing through the contents of each one, starting at the front.

There was an assortment of paperwork shoved into the front files, including copies of insurance certificates, warranties for equipment and safety inspection certificates.

In the next drawer down, I found an array of

marketing materials such as branded brochures, postcards, quotes from graphic design studios for merchandise and trade show leaflets.

I discovered that the bottom drawer was chock-full of old utility bills, letters and cards from clients thanking the team for their efforts and then, about halfway through, all the waiver forms signed by previous visitors to the activities centre.

I still hadn't found any personnel records, or anything to link Ava to whatever was going on, and crouched, idly flicking through the waiver forms while I wondered what to do next.

Then I saw a familiar name and froze.

I looked closer. Amongst the copies of waivers that previous clients had completed was one signed by Helen Dumois from four years ago. A coffee stain covered the end of her surname, and I couldn't read the full date, so I gave it a light tug and pulled it from the file. I peered at the elegant signature at the bottom of the form and then frowned as I realised that a second waiver form was stuck to the back of it, probably because the coffee stain was still wet when the forms had been gathered together at the reception desk.

I flipped over Helen's form and gently peeled away the other, holding my breath as it threatened to tear, before exhaling with relief when it came away unscathed. My heart stopped when I turned the page and read the name at the top of it though, and then the signature confirming I wasn't mistaken.

Then I heard movement outside the safe room and spun around.

Too late, my gaze fell on the gun cabinet. In my haste to look at the personnel files, I hadn't noticed that the door was ajar.

Now one of those shotguns had swung around the doorframe to point at me.

I raised my hands, the waiver forms fluttering to the concrete floor while I trembled, wondering if I had time to shout for help.

'You had to keep poking around, didn't you?' said a familiar voice. 'Just like Sarah.'

CHAPTER FORTY-ONE

'You?' I managed.

Grace Masters held the shotgun with the butt firmly tucked into her shoulder, eyeing me along the barrel with a coldness that emanated across the room to where I stood.

I was shaking, petrified while I stared at the darkened maw at the business end of it, wondering if I'd have time to duck if she pulled the trigger, and then whether I'd feel anything if I didn't.

'How did you get in?' I asked, my voice shaking.

'I saw you unlock the barn before those two policemen turned up and then when you ran and hid, I sneaked in while none of you were looking. I put the padlock back on its hasp just like you did,' she said matter-of-factly.

There was no tremor in her words, and a distinct lack of emotion.

My legs were trembling, and suddenly I wished I'd had more sense and told one of DS Drayton's colleagues where I was going.

Maybe, just maybe, if I kept her talking somebody in the house might question where we both were, especially the uniformed constable in the guest lounge who had now lost two of the people he was meant to be keeping an eye on.

'How did you get out of the house without being stopped?' I said.

'Easy.' Grace shrugged, and the barrel gave a dangerous wobble before the gun settled against her shoulder once more. 'I told the policeman I needed to go to the toilet again, and that I had an upset stomach because of the stress.'

So, that must've been at least fifteen minutes ago. Surely by now he would be knocking on the door of the lavatory just off the reception area, and if he didn't find her there, he'd make a beeline for her room.

I hoped.

'How did you get in here to get that out of the gun cabinet?' I said, my thoughts tumbling one over the other as I tried to catch up with events and wonder where on earth I got it so wrong.

'I overheard Chris tell you what the door code was on Friday when I came to let you know that dinner was ready. I figured they used the same code for the cabinet and it gave me an idea, so I changed my mind about telling you about dinner, except I accidentally caught my foot against one of the ropes out there and nearly tripped.'

So much for Chris assuring me that the scrabbling noise I'd heard was caused by the neighbourhood cat.

Grace smiled, and I shrank inside because there was no warmth there. It was predatory.

I tried lowering my hands a little because my arms were starting to ache, but Grace took a step closer and waved the shotgun at me. Terrified, I waved my hands higher, a burning sensation in my shoulders starting to take a hold. 'Tell me about Helen Dumois.'

'She didn't deserve him.'

'Who?'

'Ethan, of course. Ethan was mine.'

'Yours?'

'We'd known each other since university,' Grace explained, her tone one similar to that I'd heard parents with small children use when their patience was wearing thin. 'We went out for three months.'

I frowned. 'But you said Natasha only met him for the first time at the orienteering event last year.'

'We kept our relationship a secret. He didn't want his parents to know about us until after our finals, and then he decided he didn't want to be with me anymore and dumped me the night of our graduation ceremony.'

Ouch. That must have hurt. 'And so, when he met Helen…'

'I made sure I made friends with her,' she finished. 'I pretended it didn't matter to me. That I was happy for them.'

'Until they announced their engagement,' I guessed.

'She even asked me to be a bridesmaid.'

I think I winced. 'So, you decided to kill her on her hen weekend. Here.'

'It was an accident.'

Something clicked into place for me. 'So, when Ethan was dating again…'

'I figured I'd arrange to go to an orienteering event where I knew he'd be. I didn't want to just turn up on my own – I was worried he'd think I was stalking him or something, which of course is preposterous – so I invited Natasha along.' Grace lowered the shotgun, her eyes downcast while she recounted the story. 'She'd just had two wisdom teeth out and looked like a complete nightmare. Her face was all puffy from the bruising, but he *still* fell for her. He didn't even look at me. And then he had the cheek to ask her out.'

'And then he proposed.'

Big mistake. The shotgun swept upwards, and I tried to take a step back, but my spine smacked against the shelves of lever arch files lining the wall and I found myself staring down the gun's barrel once more.

I gulped. 'Why did you kill Sarah?'

Her brow puckered. 'I didn't want to. But she was filming us on her phone all the time this weekend, and taking photos. She didn't know it at the time, but she filmed me loosening the anchor that failed yesterday.'

'You did that?' I gasped. I had really hoped it had been an accident, despite wondering whether one of the Kingsleys had been involved, but her words made my stomach flip, and it was then I knew I wouldn't leave the room alive. 'Why?'

'Because Natasha was meant to be next up the rope and, like you, she hasn't got enough climbing experience to miss out any anchor points,' said Grace. 'But you took her place and got lucky. And then when we got to the camp site, Sarah showed me some of the videos she'd been filming, and one of them was of me sabotaging the anchor. I tried to take the phone from her so I could delete it before she realised what she had, but then Noah called us over because the food was ready, and she walked off before I could do anything.'

'But you stole her phone,' I said urgently. 'You already had what you needed. You didn't have to kill her.'

'I did,' Grace insisted, 'because she caught me stealing it. I thought she'd left her tent to go to the toilet last night, but it turned out she was just getting her travel charger from her backpack in the shelter. Her phone had gone flat. She came back and found me rummaging under her sleeping bag and told me she knew what I had done. I didn't have a choice.'

'You did have a choice,' I said. I was angry now, my fear turning to rage at the fact that two innocent lives had been taken, all because this woman was jealous of their happiness. 'You didn't have to murder either of them.'

'But I did, you see,' she said. 'Because once Natasha is dead, I'll be the only one who can console Ethan, won't I? She'll have a nasty accident, and he'll turn to his old friend seeking solace, and I'll be able to comfort him and show him what true love is.'

'You're a monster.'

'That's not nice,' she spat. In two steps, she had the barrel of the shotgun against my lips. 'You should be more careful what you say about people.'

'I'm sorry,' I mumbled, smelling the sweet aroma of gun oil, bile at the back of my throat. 'I didn't mean it.'

Grace narrowed her eyes. 'I don't believe you.'

She released the safety catch, and I closed my eyes.

CHAPTER FORTY-TWO

As I stood frozen to the spot, waiting for the shotgun's explosive release of the cartridge that would end my life, I wondered whether opting to be a private detective was the wisest decision I could have made.

I had loved my trip to India – I loved the freedom of travel, the sights and smells, and the conversations I had with total strangers. It had been an immersive experience, and the inspiration behind my career.

But it was a career that was about to come to an abrupt end in a barn in the middle of the Lake District, and all because I let myself be talked into being Natasha's bodyguard by Patricia Berriminster. I swore then that if a miracle happened and I survived this, the miscellaneous line on her invoice would include a lot more than the icepack that Heather McAdams paid for.

Right now, I could have been sitting at my desk in my little office in Bermondsey, a sushi bento box in front of me while I carried out online checks of my clients' prospective suitors, or sitting in a conference room with other fledgling investigators while we learned about new trends in counter surveillance, or…

But no.

Instead, I had the pointy end of a shotgun jabbed against my gums, which (a) hurt, and (b) was the most frightening thing I had ever been confronted by.

I knew I was going to die, and I couldn't do anything about it.

I was helpless.

'Mmmphh,' I tried.

'Shut up,' hissed Grace. 'I'm going to stop Natasha marrying Ethan, and there's nothing you can do about it.'

Holy moly, she was planning a rampage after killing me. I whimpered as I thought of the bloodshed that would follow, the lives that she would take, and choked back a sob. Tears rolled over my cheeks, and I couldn't breathe without smelling gun oil and my own fear.

'Grace,' said a calm voice, 'would you put down the gun please?'

My eyes opened to see Ava standing in the doorway, her hands held up while she tried to look as non-threatening as possible.

'I can't,' said Grace, staring at me along the barrel, her pale blue eyes as harsh as ice.

A shiver passed across my shoulders, but this time I maintained eye contact with her.

'Grace,' Ava repeated. 'Put down the gun, and let's have a chat.'

'No.'

'Okay.' Ava ventured closer, her boots making the softest of thuds on the concrete floor. 'Could you tell me what you need?'

'Stay where you are,' Grace snapped. She risked a glance over her shoulder, and then the gun pressed against my lips again. 'Don't come any closer, or she dies.'

'I'll stay here.'

I don't know how she did it, but Ava's voice didn't waver once. She was calm, exuding a confidence I bet she didn't feel, but at least she was trying.

I thought back to the training time I'd spent with Noah. If Grace had managed to fully load the shotgun before scurrying to hide somewhere in the barn until I returned, there were three cartridges inside, and she could fire them all in quick succession.

Ava wouldn't stand a chance.

'Get out,' I mumbled.

'Shut up.'

Grace smacked the end of the shotgun against my nose, and I squealed. I smelled blood a few seconds before a trickle ran over my top lip, and my eyes watered.

I saw Ava's shoulders heave as she took a deep breath, and then she tried again.

'Grace? What do you need me to do? Can I get you anything?'

'Go and get Natasha,' she snarled. 'I want her to see what she made me do.'

'Hmm,' said Ava. 'I don't think I want to leave Melody here alone. She looks frightened, doesn't she?'

'Good.' Grace's lips thinned into some semblance of a smile, but her gaze remained cold. 'She should be. She's ruined everything.'

'How?'

'She's been snooping around. She found out about Helen.'

'Who's Helen?' Ava asked. 'I haven't met her, have I?'

'She's dead.'

'How?'

'She fell. It was an accident.' Grace emitted a giggle, and my heart twisted with dread. 'That's what they said, anyway.'

'But you know the truth, is that it?' Ava said.

'Yes. I killed her.'

I saw Ava shuffle forwards again, her movements careful so as not to alert Grace, and I did my best to keep my gaze level so she wouldn't look over her shoulder. I had no idea what Ava was going to do, but if it went wrong…

'Grace,' she said. 'Ethan is here.'

Pure shock registered in Grace's eyes, and her mouth dropped open. In that split second, she loosened her grip on the shotgun, and it fell away to my left.

I saw my chance.

I lashed out, punching the soft flesh on the inside of her arm, sending a shockwave through the bone that sent her reeling, off balance. I'd trained using it time after time in the dojo, but it was the first time I'd ever used it in real life, and Grace's reaction was instantaneous.

Her hand fell open as the delicate nerves in her arm took the full force of the blow and the shotgun clattered to the floor.

At the same time, I pushed myself away from the shelves, scared that it would go off, colliding with Grace and knocking her off balance.

Ava didn't hesitate.

She launched herself at the other woman, tackling her to the ground.

Grace tried to fight back, slapping at Ava's face and growling under her breath as she wiggled and squirmed, trying to escape.

I left them to it, made my way over to where the cold steel of the shotgun barrel faced against the wall, and slipped on the safety catch and held onto it before lowering myself to the floor on shaking legs.

Then there were shouts, running feet, and the uniformed constable from the lounge and DS Drayton appeared, faces ashen.

'What's going on?' said Drayton.

I pointed at Grace, who was now subdued, her arms held behind her back by Ava, who huffed her hair from her face and glared at both the policemen.

'I don't suppose one of you is carrying a pair of handcuffs?' she said.

CHAPTER FORTY-THREE

The guest lounge was deserted when Ava and I walked in, exhausted.

An eerie silence filled the room that was only broken by the occasional crackle from the hearth as embers tumbled into the grate, displacing the charred logs that had long burned black.

It was raining again outside, and we had both been drenched walking back to the house after Grace had been taken to her room under guard. The uniformed sergeant now stood at the doorway, keeping a wary eye on her while she sat on the bed and awaited her fate.

The rain lashed against the windows, and I wandered over to peer up at the hillside looming above the activities centre, a fine mist shrouding the summit and one or two sodden sheep ambling amongst the gorse bushes.

There was no sign of Chris's four-wheel drive yet, or the police vehicles that had accompanied him back to the camp site, and I turned away from the bleak landscape to see Ava at the bar, helping herself to one of the bottles of spirits on the shelf behind it. Walking over, I pulled out one of the wooden stools and sank onto it, all the energy in my legs disappearing as the reality of the past hour caught up with me.

My heart rate was a little calmer, but nowhere near normal, and every time I closed my eyes I could see the shotgun barrel pointing at me.

I reckoned I'd be having nightmares for a while yet.

Ava slid the crystal tumbler along the bar to me, the golden liquid contents sloshing against the sides when I stopped it with my hand.

'Sip that,' she said. 'I shouldn't, professionally speaking, but in the circumstances I don't think sweetened tea is going to work, so you may as well have a short measure of brandy instead.'

'Thanks.'

I was still shaking, replaying the past hour's

events over and over in my mind, and wondering what if, what if, what if?

I was grateful no one else was around.

Isabella and Emily were in their rooms busily packing their bags and Natasha was ensconced in the kitchen, talking with DS Drayton. Two women from the forensic team were currently ransacking the barn where the rest of the shotguns were kept and reviewing the relevant licensing information under the watchful gaze of another constable. After that, they were going to inspect the equipment we had taken into the hills with us that weekend in case Grace had sabotaged anything else without our knowledge.

Meanwhile, two more of DS Drayton's constables were waiting in the rain beside one of the liveried patrol cars, ready to whisk Grace away to the police station in Barrow-in-Furness to be charged once Drayton had completed the other interviews.

I had been interviewed again as soon as we had returned to the house, explaining what I had found in the filing cabinet in the safe room, and what I had been looking for in the first place.

Drayton had listened but offered no explanations and then dismissed me while he phoned a superior officer to provide an update.

Ava had handed over both the crooked anchor pin and the empty plastic bottle still stinking of petrol to DS Drayton before steering me towards the guest lounge, and after seeing both items sealed in plastic bags resembling the sort I used for sandwiches, the penny dropped.

'You're with the police, aren't you?' I said, watching while she helped herself to a black coffee and dropped two sugar cubes into it.

She nodded, then gestured for me to follow her over to the sofas beside the fire. Taking a moment to put down her coffee mug on the table, she plucked two logs from a basket next to the hearth and placed them in the grate.

Soon, flames shot up the chimney and a fresh wave of warm air billowed into the room. I sat cradling my drink and curled up my feet underneath me while I waited for Ava to sit opposite.

She took a sip of coffee before nestling back into the cushions. 'I'm with Cumbria Police. I've been working undercover here at the activities centre for the past six weeks.'

'That explains why I couldn't find anything about you beyond three years ago,' I said, keeping Shaun Hendrick out of the conversation. 'You created a fake persona, didn't you?'

'Yes. We didn't have a lot of time to do so once we found out Natasha was going to be here this weekend. She and her friends were originally going to go to Snowdonia, but that place went bankrupt, and they had to change their plans at the last minute.'

I turned at the sound of the door opening, and then DS Drayton entered the room, weariness etched into his features. He shot a guarded smile at us by way of greeting, then spotted the steam rising from the coffee urn and made a beeline for it before wandering over to the fire.

Sitting beside Ava, he put his coffee mug on the table and clasped his hands together. 'What you did was extremely brave, Melody, but next time maybe tell me what you're planning?'

I shivered. 'Deal. So, how did you know Grace was planning to murder Natasha Berriminster?'

'I didn't,' said Drayton, then jerked his thumb at Ava. 'Someone on my team has been working some extracurricular hours on an old case and persuaded me to let her go undercover.'

I looked at her with renewed respect. 'You didn't believe the coroner's verdict about Helen, did you?'

'Helen's parents didn't accept the verdict,' Ava said, giving an embarrassed shrug. 'And when they came to me with what little findings they'd managed to collate, I asked DS Drayton if I could work the old case and conduct an audit. I saw first-hand the effect that Helen's death had on her parents. They were inconsolable and wanted answers. I wanted to help them find out the truth, once and for all.'

'Why did you have to go to Hawkshead at short notice on Friday? What was all that about?'

She contemplated her hands for a moment, then looked up. 'Isabella Kingsley contacted me shortly after I met with Helen's parents. I think they passed on my details to her and, like them, she felt that Helen's accidental death was a little too convenient. She told me how experienced Helen was, and the more I heard, the more I felt the accident had been staged to cover up a homicide. I met with Isabella on Friday before she and Emily arrived here. Isabella got in touch with me when Helen's parents told her I was reinvestigating her death. Friday was our last chance to try and work out who might've killed her before Natasha found herself in the same situation.'

'We weren't sure who the person was who killed Helen,' Ava continued, 'which made convincing others difficult. When I tabled my findings, both Chris and Noah Weller were placed under suspicion, but were later able to provide alibis. Noah has... a history with Cumbria Police but he's worked hard over the years to redress that, and both were keen to protect their reputation, which is why they allowed me to pose as a guide here. And then Patricia Berriminster got in touch with Noah and Chris a week ago, and insisted you join us to protect Natasha.'

'At which point, I agreed,' said Drayton. 'We conducted a risk assessment and decided that if there was somebody else on hand to keep an eye on Natasha, Ava could continue her investigation into proving that Grace killed Helen Dumois four years ago.'

'Was that why you were rummaging through the backpacks at the camp site last night?'

'Yes,' said Ava. 'I was trying to find that anchor before Grace tampered with it. The problem with Helen's death is that there was no evidence to prove that her life had been in danger. I wasn't going to let that happen again.'

My gaze returned to Drayton. 'You should've warned Natasha to stay away.'

'I agree, but sadly my superior officer took a different view.'

'Sarah's dead because of that.'

'I know, and I'll never forgive myself,' he said.

'You could've at least asked Patricia Berriminster to convince Natasha to do something different.'

'How?' Ava demanded. 'Would you believe us if we told you that your best friend wanted to kill you to stop you marrying her old boyfriend?'

I dropped my gaze and stared at the carpet for a moment. 'Probably not.'

'Exactly. That was the dilemma I was faced with,' Ava said. 'And I had no proof. Nothing at all. Now I've got a broken anchor and a water bottle with traces of petrol that has Grace's fingerprints on it.'

'We found Sarah's phone in her daypack too,' Drayton added. 'Grace won't get away with it this time – Sarah managed to film her tampering with the anchor while she was climbing the cliff before you yesterday. She'll be going away for a very long time.'

'They should throw away the key,' I replied, before turning my attention to Ava. 'And how come you didn't say anything? You could've warned me.'

'Until today, everybody that came into contact with Natasha was perceived as a threat,' she said. 'Sorry, but the risk assessment for this operation made that necessary.'

After a moment I sighed, drained the last of the brandy, and rose to my feet. 'Am I free to go?'

'Until we call you as a witness for the prosecution

or have more questions about this weekend, yes,' said Drayton. He stood, walked around the table and held out his hand. 'Thank you. We'll be in touch.'

I shook his hand and then turned to Ava. 'Thanks for saving my life back there. That was brave.'

'You're welcome,' she said. 'I hope your client's wedding goes well.'

I followed them from the lounge and then looked through the open front door at the sound of tyres to see Chris's four-wheel drive sweep into the yard, closely followed by two of the police Land Rovers.

Drayton and Ava walked outside to meet them, and I watched in silence as one of the patrols climbed out of their vehicle and moved to the back, opening the door before manhandling the stretcher we had made to carry Noah to the camp site yesterday.

There was a slight form under a familiar blue sleeping bag on it now, but I could see the black plastic poking out from under it, and my heart sank at the realisation it was a body bag, and that Sarah Llewellyn would now start her final journey back to her hometown.

I looked over my shoulder at the sound of a loud sniff to see Natasha standing between Emily and Isabella Kingsley at the kitchen door, the three women clinging to each other while tears streamed down their faces.

I clenched my fists, digging my nails into my palms before turning away.

It was time for me to go.

CHAPTER FORTY-FOUR

I closed the door to my room and rested my forehead against the uneven wooden surface before closing my eyes.

Outside in the hallway, I could hear a pair of male voices – DS Drayton and one of his constables by the sound of it – but they were speaking too low for me to make out the words. Then a door slammed shut somewhere further along, and I straightened, trying to ignore the dizzy sensation that seized me.

I recognised the signs of hunger, but I couldn't face eating anything. Noah had tried coaxing me to at least have a sandwich before I'd retreated to my room, but my stomach flipped and bile rose to my throat at the thought, and I'd pleaded for a mug of tea instead, assuring him I would eat something once I had finished packing.

I turned to face the room, taking in the narrow bed, the plain pinewood wardrobe and the matching bedside table. I'd left my current read behind yesterday, figuring I wouldn't have time to lose myself in a book while hiking around the Lakes, and flicked absently through the pages, the words blurring before my eyes.

My backpack was at the foot of the bed, unopened since we had returned to the activities centre four hours ago and placed there by one of the policemen while we had been ushered to the guest lounge. I ran my hand over it and shivered, knowing I would sell it online when I got back to London rather than have the constant reminder of what had happened this weekend.

I took a deep breath and sank onto the bed, smoothing down the folds in the duvet while I looked out the window and watched the forensic specialists packing up their van, their movements methodical.

They turned towards the gate blocking the yard at the same time I heard a car engine purr to a standstill and got up to see a taxi idling at the entrance to the activities centre, its headlights on in the encroaching twilight.

A man climbed out wearing a three-quarter-length wool coat over blue jeans and rugged boots, opened a black umbrella and then beckoned to one of the forensic technicians while the taxi driver turned the car around.

I realised this must be Natasha's father, Peter Berriminster.

He shared the same dark hair with his daughter, although as he walked past my window I could see the peppering of silver at his temples and deep brow lines. His jaw was set as he stooped to listen to the technician that accompanied him, then gave a curt nod. The entrance to the house was beyond my line of sight, but I heard the front door slam shut and then DS Drayton's voice.

I cracked open my door a little in time to hear a relieved sob, and Natasha's exclamation.

'You're here,' she said, her relief evident. 'Thank goodness.'

Their voices faded into the guest lounge, and I went back to the bed, stripping off my damp clothes before moving to the tiny en suite and standing under the shower while hot water gushed over my head.

The roar of the hairdryer drowned out my thoughts for a few minutes, and then once I was dressed in my favourite jeans, black-sleeved base layer top and a burgundy-coloured sweatshirt that I'd had since university, I hoisted my backpack over my shoulder and gave the room a once-over in case I'd forgotten anything.

I picked up the paperback for the return train journey.

I didn't want to open my laptop and read all the messages that would surely be waiting for me.

Wandering down the hallway towards the front door, I saw Natasha and her father emerge from the lounge ahead of DS Drayton. They stopped, and she pointed to me.

'Dad, this is Melody Harper.'

He strode towards me with such intent that I took a step back before he caught up with me and enveloped me in a bear hug.

'Thank you,' he said. He pulled away, and I saw the tears in his eyes. 'Thank you for looking out for her.'

'That's okay,' I mumbled, feeling my cheeks redden.

'Anything you need,' he continued, his hands still on my arms. 'Anything at all, you only need to ask. I've got some very influential friends and business colleagues. I owe you.'

'Dad.' Natasha moved closer to him and rested a hand on his. 'You're embarrassing her.'

'Oh, of course.' He smiled and looked a little contrite. 'I'm just so grateful.'

'It's okay,' I repeated. 'And thank you.'

Peter Berriminster gave a small nod, then put an arm around his daughter's shoulder. 'Right, where are your keys? Let's get you home. Your mother's beside herself with worry.'

He fussed over her for a few minutes more, insisting on carrying her bags out to her four-wheel drive before returning, umbrella in hand to escort her to the vehicle. I got the impression he was afraid of something else happening before he could whisk her away, worry etched into his features as he waited for her to say goodbye to Ava, Noah and Chris.

I wandered outside and stood under the porch while she pulled on her boots. The rain had stopped but left behind enormous puddles that pooled between the cracks in the concrete hardstanding that rippled with the wind.

'I'll be with you in a minute, Dad,' said Natasha.

He raised an eyebrow but then handed her the umbrella and jogged across to the four-wheel drive, the indicators flashing once as he aimed the key fob at it before climbing in and starting the engine.

'Listen.' Natasha turned to me, tugging at my sleeve and taking me to one side, away from the others. 'I need to thank you. They should've told both of us what was going on.'

'You don't have to thank me,' I insisted. 'I was doing my job.'

'You saved my life.' She shivered. 'If I'd climbed that rope yesterday... If you hadn't smelled the petrol last night...'

'But you're okay,' I said. 'I'm so sorry about Sarah. Have you had a chance to speak with her parents?'

'Yes,' she said, eyes red from crying. 'The police sent a liaison officer to their house to tell them. They're in a bad way. I'm going to go and see them in the morning.'

'And the wedding?'

'I wanted to cancel it, so did Ethan, but Sarah's mum and dad didn't want me to. They've said I need to go ahead, because that's what she would've wanted.'

'That's incredibly nice of them to say so.'

'It is, isn't it?' She managed a watery smile.

I looked back at a shout from one of the police constables who were shepherding Isabella and Emily to their vehicle. It was almost dark now, and I needed to be on my way, heading back to Windermere before the last train left for my London-bound journey. Turning to Natasha, I held out my hand, and she paused before shaking it. 'I should say congratulations for next weekend.'

'Thank you,' she said. 'For everything.'

'I'll give your mum a call tomorrow to give her all the details. I'm sure you're exhausted, and maybe it'll help in some little way to let you grieve in peace rather than have to relive it.'

'Thanks.'

I walked away, casting my gaze around the yard to find Chris and ask him for a lift back to Windermere, when Natasha called after me.

'Melody?'

I turned. 'Yes?'

'Would you like to come to the wedding?'

CHAPTER FORTY-FIVE

There wasn't a dry eye in the house.

Or church, I should say.

The weather was even behaving itself, with a bright cloudless sky bathed in indigos and blues framing the Wiltshire village and a rare warmth that hadn't been seen for nearly a month. Beyond the church there was a small woodland and the last of the oak and beech leaves were adding a golden halo to the churchyard, casting a soft light over the ancient yew tree in the corner beside the nave and illuminating the stained-glass windows.

Patricia and Peter Berriminster had arranged for a marquee to be erected in the tiny car park outside the church, within which a catering company prepared canapés and champagne for the guests, and a chocolate fountain for the various children who were running around, their giggles and screams of laughter filling the air.

The sound of the church organ carried through the building as we threw rice paper confetti over Ethan and Natasha when they emerged from the fourteenth-century building, man and wife.

Natasha looked amazing, of course. Wary, a little paler than when I'd first met her, but smiling for the photographer while holding hands with her five-year-old niece who was acting as flower girl for the ceremony.

There was a loud sniff next to me, and I glanced over to see my plus-one, Charlie, wiping his eyes with the sleeve of his borrowed suit jacket.

'This is just beautiful,' he said, followed by another sniff. 'Innit?'

'It is.' I grinned and opened the glitter-covered handbag I'd purchased on sale and at the last minute. 'Do you want a tissue?'

'Ta.'

He blew his nose with such force that two of Natasha's elderly aunties in front of us visibly jumped, and one of Ethan's ushers peered over their heads with an ill-disguised frown.

I ignored them, too relieved to care what they thought. Natasha was here, she had married the man of her dreams, and she was safe.

Both she and Ethan had taken a moment at the end of the ceremony to pay tribute to Sarah, Natasha battling through her speech with a wobble in her voice while her husband held her hand, his head lowered. Sarah's parents had been in the front pew with Patricia and Peter Berriminster, while Isabella and Emily sat and listened, their poise stoic.

Now, I looked around at the sound of my name to see a large man heading towards me with the countenance of a bull. I'd recognised Seamus Kingsley when he had joined Ethan and the ushers at the altar when they had first arrived at the church and held out my hand as he drew near.

He ignored it, and like Peter Berriminster only a few days before, enveloped me into a hug that knocked the air from my lungs and made my eyes water.

'Isabella and I can't thank you enough,' he gushed. 'We'll always be forever in your debt.'

'That's really not necessary,' I squeaked, extricating myself as gently as possible before taking a deep breath.

'It is.' He wagged a stern finger at me. 'And mark

my words, I'll be recommending your business to my colleagues, Miss Harper. I mean that.'

'Thank you.'

'Hang on.' Seamus looked over his shoulder and beckoned to one of the catering staff who were walking around carrying silver trays laden with bubbling champagne flutes.

'Here,' he said, handing one to each of us. 'Have this while it's still cold. There's nothing more depressing than warm fizz.'

He helped himself to a glass, then clinked it against ours.

'To Sarah,' I said.

'Yes, to Sarah,' he replied gravely.

There was a moment's silence, and then one of the guest's children tore past us, his jacket stretched out behind him while he made aeroplane noises.

'You'll be joining us at the reception, yes?' Seamus looked from me to Charlie, who fiddled with his cufflinks under Seamus's inspection.

'Sorry, this is my friend, Charlie Zervas,' I said, 'and yes, we'll be at the reception.'

'Good, good.' He glanced over his shoulder at a shout from Isabella. 'Right, must go. Duty calls.'

I smiled and watched him weave his way through

the crowd with a bounce in his step towards Ethan and Noah, and the photographer started herding the wedding party together for a series of poses that would no doubt end up being published in one of the society glossies by the end of the year.

'Reception?' said Charlie, turning to me. 'Hope they've got a disco.'

'I can't dance,' I grimaced. 'I'll just watch.'

'How can you have a black belt in karate and not dance?' he demanded. 'It's just footwork patterns. Dancing is like katas – without the punching of course.'

I spluttered, almost choking on the champagne. 'Now I'll never get that vision out of my head.'

'Here, hold this.' He handed me his glass. 'Need the loo. Back in a minute.'

I wandered over to a wooden bench beside the yew tree, placed the glasses on the ground beside it and sat, enjoying the sun's warmth on my face while I watched Natasha's friends and family fuss around her. She had chosen pink and white flowers for her bouquets and Ethan and his ushers wore buttonholes in the same colours, their ties chosen to match the dusky pink bouquet petals that poked through tendrils of delicate ivy.

Squirming under the scrutiny of strangers, many of whom were casting surreptitious looks my way or openly pointing at me, I clutched my bag in my lap and forced myself not to check my mobile phone as a way to avoid their gaze.

I saw a flash of red out of the corner of my eye and followed it along the tree line beyond the centuries-old gravestones until a break in the foliage revealed a brightly coloured narrowboat cruising along the canal beyond the churchyard. A couple stood side by side at the tiller, watching the wedding party with interest, and somewhere I heard a dog emit an excited *yip* before they slipped from sight.

Leaning back against the wooden bench, I felt my shoulders start to relax for the first time in days. In addition to DS Drayton calling to double check facts and let me have updates where he could, my phone hadn't stopped ringing with new enquiries from prospective clients, many of whom I suspected were friends of the Kingsleys and the Berriminsters.

Both families had stayed true to their word and were extolling my efforts at thwarting Grace's plans to murder Natasha, and I was struggling to cope with the number of potential clients I was having to deal with.

I was having a change of heart about my office arrangements too.

I hadn't yet broken the news to Charlie but after the open ruggedness of the Lake District, my office and tiny rented apartment seemed cramped and claustrophobic on my return to London, and I was starting to wonder if it was time for a change of scenery.

Driving through the Wiltshire countryside with Charlie on the way to the wedding earlier today, I realised that I could live somewhere like this and still maintain a client base in London if I wanted to. There was a mainline railway station not too far away that would deliver me to either Paddington or Waterloo in under two hours, and renting was cheaper here too. Plus, I could keep myself distanced from some of the people I was investigating.

Just in case.

I jumped as a shadow fell over me, then squinted up at a woman in her late sixties who was eyeing me with interest.

She wore a cream-coloured skirt suit and a matching hat with a sprig of wildflowers tucked under the ribbon. She checked over her shoulder to where Seamus and Isabella Kingsley stood talking with the vicar before turning back to me.

'Excuse me, it's Melody isn't it?'

'Yes.'

'Can we talk in private?' She didn't wait and instead wrapped her fingers around my arm and steered me past the marquee tent and the chocolate fountain, side-stepping a six-year-old boy who had escaped his mother's watchful eye and was dipping his whole hand into the gooey mixture before licking his fingers. She stopped behind one of the marquee pillars that had been decorated with pink and white roses to match Natasha's bouquet and glanced over her shoulder. 'This will have to do.'

'Look, I'm sorry, but who are you?'

'I'm Lisa.' Her eyes widened then, and she let go of my arm. 'I'm so sorry.'

'It's okay. Something's obviously bothering you, and you know who I am, so how can I help you?'

Lisa swallowed, then took a deep breath. 'I've got a job for you, although it's something a little different from what you're used to. Would you be interested?'

I thought back to the events of the past week, the losses that had been endured by Helen and Sarah's families, then watched as Ethan and Natasha walked towards their waiting limousine to be whisked to the reception hotel, cheered on by their family and friends.

Finally, I turned back to Lisa and smiled. 'What do you need me to do?'

THE END

ABOUT THE AUTHOR

Before turning to writing, USA Today bestselling crime author Rachel Amphlett played guitar in bands, worked as a TV and film extra, dabbled in radio as a presenter and freelance producer for the BBC, and worked in publishing as an editorial assistant.

She now wields a pen instead of a plectrum and writes crime fiction with over 30 novels and short stories featuring spies, detectives, vigilantes, and assassins.

A keen traveller and accidental private investigator, Rachel has both Australian and British citizenship.

Find out more at www.rachelamphlett.com.